RENEE

A West Bay Novel
Book One

Author
T. L. Nelson

This book is a work of fiction. Any names or characters, businesses or places, events, or incidents, are fictitious, or a product of the author's imagination. Any resemblance to actual persons, living or dead, or actual events is purely coincidental.

Front and back cover picture -
[URL=http://www.tokkoro.com/3105019

Every drug addict has similar characteristics, but not all have the same experience. Some may try hard drugs one time and never go back to them, while others can use them from time to time and never become addicted. Then there are the ones we hear about the most. Their addiction has overcome them to the point that, no matter how many times they desperately try to heal, they can't climb out of the grave they have dug. It is a living hell for them and their family.

Dedicated to my one client. You are missed, my friend.

Acknowledgments

Thomas J. Harvey (contributor)
No words can express my <u>unending gratitude</u> for your
help, editing skills, and total support, and advice about,
well, everything.
My family - Victoria and Vincent Reilly, John Nelson.

Chris Nelson - you always believed in me for doing
this.
Janet Richmond - for your honest opinion. An
awesome sister in Christ and cousin.
Zachary Thomasson - for your opinions, and advice,
and always being there.
Chuck Pew - for the name 'Illusive.'
Benjamin McCall - answering my many questions
about publishing this book.
The several people that I had talked with about their
addictions and all the information they gave me.
And
JESUS CHRIST
My savior! The one I live for, who keeps me going,
and kept me positive through this whole writing process.
What a learning
experience. Amen.

RENEE

T. L. Nelson

Chapter One

West Bay Avenue, located on Queens Shore's north side, was well known for its posh boutiques, cafes, and a one-of-a-kind view of the bay. Renee Nolan had visited the avenue on occasion, but she had never been to the area where she was heading to for a job interview.

The moment she turned onto Queens Shores Drive, her eyes widened in awe of the extravagant homes. She followed the curve of the road and grinned noticing a cherry red Escalade parked in a driveway. His driveway. She would take a Cadillac over the Porsche and Mercedes that sat across the street any day, including the Bentley that sat a few houses up.

Jaylon MacKie paced the living room floor as he talked on the phone and in the same heated argument before Renee called about the job. He thought he heard someone walk onto the porch, so he pulled the curtain back just enough to see out.

She took a deep breath and exhaled to calm her nerves. When her fingertip touched the doorbell, the door swung open, and his eyes met her eyes. He looked familiar to her, but she wasn't going to assume the fine-looking man was who she thought he was.

He pressed the end call button on his phone and said, "You must be Renee Nolan."

"Yes. I am."

"Come in. We can talk in the dining room," he said, thinking that she looked familiar, as well.

His home was warm and inviting. Handsome woodwork and rich colors accented the walls which she loved, but what caught her eye was a den with several shelves, cluttered with books.

A Cadillac and a book junkie. My kind of man, she thought.

Moments later, he noticed she wasn't behind him, so he went back and stood next to her. Most of the time she didn't like for someone to stand too close to her, but the warmth of his body and a slight hint of his cologne made her smile.

"That's quite a collection," she said.

"Spending time in vintage bookstores is a hobby of mine." He looked at her and said, "Follow me."

He pulled out a chair from the dining room table. "Have a seat. This is the first time I've placed an ad for a housekeeper, or anything else for that matter."

When he sat down across from her, she gasped as her attention was jerked away to the sound of a door slamming shut.

"It's just me, Jaylon!" a lady said.

"That's my mother. I'm sorry if she startled you." He put his bare foot on top of his knee, scratched his scruffy chin, and yawned. He then noticed a sheet of paper that she was holding.

"Is that your resume?"

"Yes," she said, and she handed it to him.

He glanced over it and said, "You're from upstate New York."

"That's right."

"You cleaned a few homes and worked for a security company," he said as if he knew of the company.

"Despite the background checks and drug testing, it turned out to be a good job," she said candidly.

Jaylon never liked it when people tried to impress him, and by the tone of her comment, he thought she was doing just that.

In the meantime, his mother came from the back room and heard them talking.

"Is that your way of saying I don't need to do a background check?" he asked point blank. And then his brow furrowed. "And you live at 20th and Ocean View Drive."

She wasn't quite sure what to think of his change in demeanor, but instead of speaking up, like she usually would have, she kept quiet.

His mother rolled her eyes, and muttered, "Jaylon you may be tired, but your attitude stinks."

He scanned through the rest of her resume and looked up only to see cold eyes staring back at him.

"Excuse me?" She said with a slight New York accent. "I may not live on your side of the street, but Ocean View Drive isn't exactly the Projects." And she snatched her resume right from his hands. "You might try using some tact on the next person you interview because this one is over." And she stormed toward the door.

He ran his hand through his hair, frustrated. "Wait. I'm sorry. I'm not doing very well here."

She stopped and turned. "No, you're not."

"Your resume looks really good. I'd like to show you my

home, so you will know what to expect. That is if you want the job."

"That's a big if," his mother mumbled.

"That's a big if," Renee said as she glanced toward the den and then back at him. "All right, lead the way."

His mother didn't want to disturb them, so she hurried to the back room.

Renee tried to get a better look at the house, but her eyes kept creeping back to the six-foot view in front of her. Yup, he does have a fine home, she thought.

The moment they entered the kitchen, she was in awe. Rich wood grain cabinets adorned the walls, exquisite tile flooring, and a six-burner stove with a double oven.

He saw the spark in her eyes as she gazed at the oven. "I take it you like to bake. Maybe you can remedy that."

His mother laughed under her breath. "You better sweeten your attitude for that to happen."

"Come on, let's head upstairs," he said.

Renee smiled and followed him.

He showed her the first three bedrooms, and then he led her down the hallway.

"This is my room." Soft hues and beige undertones gave off a relaxed feeling while long flowing curtains outlined the panoramic view of the city and the bay.

"Fantastic view," she said.

"My wife loved this room. She called it her sanctuary."

She looked at him wondering why he referred to his wife in past tense.

When they headed back down the hallway, she noticed an enclosed glass frame that contained gold and platinum albums, and CDs, along with a picture of the rock band Illusive. A slight grin came over her face, as she knew exactly who he was. But then her smile faded, knowing her daughter Chloe would have loved to have seen this, as well.

"Precious items there," he said, with a proud grin. "Let's go back down to the dining room."

As they sat at the table, he slid a sheet of paper across to her. "This is a list of everything I have told you, and it explains a few other details, as well."

She scanned it over but stopped halfway down. "You are paying six hundred a week and a bonus if I have to stay late?"

He smiled and sat back. "That's two hundred a day, for three days. It's the going rate around here. The job is yours if you want it." She was too boggled by the amount of money he was going to pay her that she didn't reply right away. He then noticed the diamond ring on her finger. "Why don't you talk it over with your husband."

She looked up at him. "My husband?"

"You didn't mention that you are married on your resume. You can let me know tomorrow. Just don't call too early."

"It won't be a problem. Really."

"Look. I have no doubt you can do the job." He rubbed his eyes with his fingertips trying to figure out how to say what he really meant. "I'm not sure how to say this without sounding like an egotistical jerk, but I just want to be sure he doesn't have any problems with you working for me, especially if you have to stay late."

"I am more than sure it will not be a problem."

"Good. I hope to hear from you."

"Wait. I didn't get your name."

Though it was an honest mistake on his part, he could tell by the way she looked at the glass frame that she knew who he was. "I'm sorry. I wasn't thinking. I'm Jaylon MacKie."

"Ok, Mr. MacK—"

"Jaylon. Just call me Jaylon.

She smiled. "I'll let you know tomorrow."

After she left, he went back to the kitchen where his mother was leaning against the counter and grinning.

"What?" he asked, chuckling.

"You about missed out on having fresh baked bread," she said. "I need to get home."

He laughed and said, "I'll talk to you later."

The next morning Renee dressed into her running clothes, slid her purple Saucony running shoes on, and headed to Maury's Diner.

"Here ya go, sweetie. Two eggs, two pieces of bacon, and two biscuits," Marla said to Renee. She then filled her mug with coffee and left.

Renee put the mug against her lips and inhaled the rich aroma. After a few sips, she heard Marla talking over the bustling hum of the café. "Hey there good looking. About time you come home."

Renee directed her eyes up and saw the back of a man and his wavy blond hair. Jaylon MacKie.

"I'll have your coffee ready in a second, hon," Marla said to him.

"No hurry," he said. He looked around the diner and spotted Renee sitting over by the window. "Mind if I join you?"

She shrugged her shoulders. "Did you check my references?" she asked, point-blank.

He returned a blunt look. "Excuse me?"

"I just might be a bad person, because of where I live."

Marla brought over a fresh pot of coffee. "This place is hopping," she said, filling his mug to the brim. "Now, what can I get for ya?"

"I'll have what she's having."

In the meantime, Ricky Carlyle walked into the diner and talking on his phone. He had a seat in a booth across from them, and every few seconds he would glance over at Renee.

Ricky was a smooth talker. The moment he moved to Queens Shores, he had the local drug scene attached to him like a magnet. From the dirt poor to the filthy rich, and social elect, he had a way of getting people under his thumb, just like the devil himself.

"What do you mean by that?" Jaylon asked Renee.

She almost laughed, knowing that she had insulted him.

Jaylon didn't laugh, but he did notice how Ricky kept darting his eyes their way.

Marla came back with Jaylon's breakfast. "Here ya go, sweetie."

When she set the bill on the table, Jaylon asked, "Who is the guy sitting in the booth behind you? He has been staring at us ever since you took my order."

Renee was too busy enjoying her breakfast that she didn't hear what Jaylon had asked Marla.

Marla took a quick glance at him. "He comes in quite often. I think his name is Ricky. Not sure, though. He doesn't talk much to anyone here, and he is always talking on his phone." She then smiled, and said, "You two enjoy your breakfast."

"Thank you, Marla." He then turned his attention back to Renee. "Anyway. Did you talk to your husband?"

Renee grinned. "Sounds like you really want me to work for you. Or you're desperate."

"Desperate? I don't think so." He chuckled. "Picky might be the word."

Renee downed the last drop of her coffee and picked up her receipt. "I need to be going. I have cleaning supplies to buy." She stood up and said, "Oh, by the way, you don't have to worry about my husband. He's cool with it."

He snatched the receipt from her hand. "I've got this. I'll see you Monday."

"Thank you. See you Monday."

He's cool with it. Stupid thing to say, she thought as she left the diner.

Jaylon sighed with a slight grin. There was something about her he liked, but he just wished he knew where he had seen her before. He then glanced over at Ricky, and his smile faded.

Ricky darted a snide look at him and then turned his attention back to his phone.

Breakfast at Maury's always left Renee feeling stuffed, and this time she was too stuffed to go for a run so soon after eating. So instead, she drove to the local department store for the cleaning supplies only to get sidetracked by several new styles of running shoes.

Two hours later, she left with a pair of purple and wild green Saucony running shoes, and cleaning supplies. She then headed to the edge of Bay Park.

After a quick stretch, she began a slow jog along the dirt path. The breeze off the bay was perfect, and she picked up the pace

Thirty minutes later, she turned to go back, and a white car veered towards her. She gasped and jumped back onto the grass as the car speed away. There is no way driver didn't see me, she thought as she continued running back to her car.

Chapter Two

Renee washed two Vicodin pain pills down with the coffee that had brewed a few hours ago. Nothing like cold coffee, she thought, knowing relief was on the way. An all too familiar pain awoke her during the night, as the OTC pain meds were not doing their job.

"Now to call Jaylon," she muttered, seeing that it was two p.m. In the three months she had worked for him, she had never been late.

"You're late," Jaylon answered impatiently. "I hope you're on your way. I need to leave soon, and you don't have a key to get in."

"Maybe you should do something about that," she said hintingly. "I'm on my way. Something showed its ugly face and had to be taken care of."

"Just get here as soon as you can," he said, and he hung up.

"Well, that went over good," she mumbled while flipping through the TV channels only to stop on a Christian network.

A lady preacher was talking about how God will give you an abundance of hope. "Hope," she sighed as she wiggled her wedding rings off and set them on the coffee table. Right then she heard a sharp knock on the door.

She looked through the peep-hole. A man with dark hair and a police officer was standing at her door. She kept the chain on the door and opened it.

The dark-haired man showed her his badge and said, "I'm detective Leary. I'm working with Seattle's FBI department, and this is Sergeant Maly from Queens Shores Police Department. "Are you Mrs. Renee Cready?"

"I'm Renee Nolan. Cready was my married name."

Detective Leary slid his sunglasses on top of his head. "This is a matter that needs to be discussed in private."

Mr. TV detective, she thought as she sucked her jowls in to keep from grinning at the hardened gel holding his hair in place. "I'm already late for work." His impatient look told her he could care less. "Ok. We can talk outside."

"Mrs. Cready—"

"Renee."

"We have personal information about your family. I don't think your neighbors need to hear what we have to say. We'll try not to take too much of your time."

"Ok." She reluctantly let them come inside, and they had a seat on the sofa, and she sat in the recliner across from them. "Now, what's this about." Though she probably knew why they wanted to talk to her, she sure wasn't expecting to hear what they were about to tell her.

"We have been trying to locate you. You made yourself hard to find," Detective Leary said.

"You could have found me sooner if you really wanted to."

"Boston Police Department has been investigating an organized crime operation that runs through several U.S. cities;

10

Boston, New York, Chicago, Los Angeles, and Seattle. We have some pictures that we would like for you to look at."

"As I told you, I'm already late for work, and my boss is not the least bit patient today."

"This shouldn't take too long."

He opened a large manila envelope, pushed her wedding rings to the side, and laid four photos on the coffee table. "Do any of these guys look familiar?"

"Nope."

"Take your time."

She looked again. "No," she said adamantly.

Sergeant Maly furrowed his eyebrows. "You've never seen these people? They played a big part in the operation. We have proof that your husband was involved with these men."

"You have got to be kidding. No. My husband wasn't involved with drugs, the mafia, or anything like that. He didn't even drink or smoke. You've got the wrong person. You're wasting your time, and you need to leave," she said as she walked over to the door.

"Please listen to what we have to say. This is very important," Detective Leary said.

"Why should I listen to you? What new information can you shed light on that will only lead to nothing?"

"Give us a few more minutes of your time, and then we will leave."

"Make it a quick few more minutes," she said and sat back down.

"Thank you. You and your husband was married for fifteen years. Did you know anything about him before the two of you met?" Detective Leary asked. She shook her head no. "The organization, Carlyle Mission, formed in 1985. Your husband joined three years later."

"My husband was not involved in anything like this. We

11

stayed to ourselves, minded our own business, and had two children. We were just a normal family."

He set another picture on the table. "Is this your husband?"

She took a quick glance. "No."

"Are you sure? Take a closer look."

She looked again. But this time, she kept quiet as she stared at the picture in disbelief. This guy had the same grey-blue eyes as her husband, but his hair was dark brown, and his nose and chin were different. He looked evil. There was no way this man was her late husband and the father of her children.

"This can't be Paul. Paul wasn't . . ." She turned the picture over, unable to speak.

"I know this is a shock to you," Sergeant Maly said, turning the picture back over. He then set another one beside it. "Your husband went by the name of Nick Castle. He was an assistant to this guy, Mason Lenherst. Mason was in charge of drug trafficking and a few other details. He would send your husband out to do his dirty work, and even kill if necessary."

She snapped a look at him. "This is absurd!"

He cut her off quickly before she could say anything else. "Lenherst is dead, as well as these two," he said, gesturing to their picture. He then laid another one beside it. "And this man, Carl Serelley, is in prison for life. He is one of the two that murdered your family. He described your husband to a T. We are looking for the other one."

"We are coming up on the short end for leads," Detective Leary said. "We thought you might be able to help us."

"That is not my husband! He wasn't involved with these people, and his name wasn't Nick Castle." It was all she could do to stay calm. "And after all this time, you're just now coming to me with this? I don't understand. I wanted answers. I wasted a lot of money on a private investigator."

"Think about it, Renee. What are the odds of someone

breaking into your home and killing your family for no reason? You blew their murder off as a freak thing, never to think of it again, and then you moved away. Your husband was allowed to leave the organization with the understanding that he never mentions it to anyone, ever, or he would be killed. Hence, the change of identity."

"Then why would they come after him years later?" And right then, it sunk in. "He messed up, or something went wrong, and..." She shook her head no trying to understand. "Wait. I was supposed to be in the house, too. Then why didn't they come after me sooner if they wanted me dead, as well?"

"I don't know." He sighed. "Maybe waiting for the perfect time, hoping the investigation would go away. Besides, you hid from just about everyone."

"I stayed out of sight because I was afraid. Someone goes into your home and knocks your family off tends to put questions in your head. Makes you keep your eyes open. I got tired of living that way. Hence, I moved," she said, aggravated. She walked over to the door and opened it. "Please leave. Now."

Detective Leary handed her his card. "I'm sorry. If you remember anything at all, no matter what it is, please let me know. You can contact Sergeant Maly at the police department, as well." And they left.

She grabbed the blanket from the top of the sofa and wrapped it around her. This can't be, she thought as tears slipped down her face, and she drifted off to sleep, but only for a moment, as someone else was knocking on her door.

"Who is it this time?" she mumbled, opening the door.

"Here's a key to my house," Jaylon said impatiently.

"Thank you." And she took the key.

He then noticed her swollen eyes and knew something was wrong. He relaxed his mood, and said, "You're welcome. See you later."

She slumbered back to the sofa, picked up her wedding rings, and held them against her heart. "I miss you all so much," she muttered.

A half hour had passed when she begrudgingly left to go to Jaylon's house

Cars streamed along like a mad river during West Bays rush hour, but the hectic traffic didn't phase her. She was numb from everything that the detective and the police officer had told her about her husband, which made the regular twenty-minute drive to Jaylon's house seem even longer.

"Finally," she said, pulling into his driveway.

When she had finished cleaning downstairs, she took a quick break and grabbed a coke from the fridge. "I should've taken the day off, or quit," she said as she looked up the stairway. "Two years free of this pain that has no rhyme, or reason, or name, and now it's back." She downed the last of the coke. "Breaks over."

Bolts of pain shot up her legs as she climbed the stairs. "I've got to find a pain specialist, and sooner than soon."

Upon reaching the landing, she gazed at the glass frame that contained the gold and platinum albums and CDs. She had promised to take her daughter to one of Jaylon's concerts, but that was one promise that never came to fruition.

An hour later, after she had finished cleaning Jaylon's room, she took a moment to look out at the bay. The sun's warm glow made her feel calm and relaxed, so much so that she didn't notice Jaylon pulling into the driveway.

Jaylon got out of his vehicle and noticed several CDs lying in the front seat of her car. "She really is a fan," he said to himself, and suddenly, he got an idea. Moments later, he went inside.

"Renee, I'm back!" he said, shutting the kitchen door with

his foot.

The delicious aroma of pizza reminded her that she had not eaten today. "Hi. I'm going to get on home," she said as she came down-stairs.

He couldn't help but notice her weary appearance. "Are you ok? You look pale."

"I'm fine. I just need to go home."

"I brought a pizza home. I'd like for you to stay and eat." He grinned. "Please."

"I am rather hungry." She chuckled. "Besides, I hate to see man plead."

He laughed and grabbed a couple of plates and sodas and set them on the table. "So, did you get everything taken care of earlier." She looked at him confused. "Are you saying your husband has an ugly face?" he quipped, referring to the comment she made on the phone.

"Excuse me?"

"You're not wearing your wedding rings."

"Oh," she laughed. "I'm not married. It was time to take them off. You wear something for years and —"

"Yeah. I know what you mean." He set his coke can down and leaned back in his chair. "My wife Leighanna died of ovarian cancer three years ago. I keep our wedding rings in a safe, and on occasion, I take them out just to look at them. I've kept a few of her clothes, as well. She even had a shirt like the one you're wearing. Black with a red rose imprinted on it." He leaned forward and crossed his arms on the table. "So are you divorced, or..." and he stopped talking, realizing his question was not in the best of taste, nor did it come out the way he meant it to.

She quickly downed her soda. "I need to go. Thanks for the pizza."

"I'm sorry. That is really none of my business. I didn't

mean to upset you."

"No reason to be sorry. It's just hard to talk about that part of my life."

"I understand. And I'm sorry about being so hateful earlier."

"You're my boss and needed me here."

"You're calling me boss, again." She grinned. "By the way, there have been reports of kids breaking into cars, so you might want to keep your car locked when you come here."

"Thanks for the warning," she said. "I'll see you in a few days."

The moment she got inside her car, she noticed that her Illusive CDs were lying in the order they had been recorded. She picked one up and then the others. He had autographed all of them. She then looked up only to see him standing at the dining room window grinning. Her face blushed. She had never told him that she was a fan of his music.

"Right, kids breaking into cars," she laughed as she drove away.

Three

Mikes Pub is located a few blocks south of Ocean View Drive. Renee was not one to go to bars, but Mike's Pub was quiet, and people minded their own business there. And, not only that, Mike grills up the tastiest hamburgers and mega side of seasoned fries.

The leader of the rhythm and blues band nodded at Renee as she sat in her usual seat at the bar. She returned a smile, and the band began to play to a smooth beat.

Mike drew her usual diet coke from the fountain and set it on a small napkin in front of her. "Where ya been lately? Carmen and I have missed you." Mike and his wife Carmen befriended Renee not long after she started frequenting the pub.

"Just been busy." She sipped on the coke, and then said, "You know, I think I'll try something different tonight. Maybe vodka mixed with a bit of something sweet."

He shoved his dark hair off his face. "You celebrating something?" he asked, shocked. He had never known her to drink.

"Nope." She watched him mix the orange pop with vodka and then top it off with a swirl of whipped cream. "Well, I did find a job."

"That's a good reason to celebrate. Where at?"

"Queens Shore Drive. Housekeeping."

"Oooh, West Bay." She snickered at him. "Big money." She raised her eyebrows and grinned. "Congratulations. It's on me." He set the drink on a fresh napkin and went to the other end of the bar.

She took a slow sip, and then another, feeling the ting as it slid down her throat. She smiled. Twenty years didn't make a difference.

Several minutes later, Mike came back, and she said, "One more time."

"Just one more, eh?" And he refilled her glass.

The band slowed to a relaxing bass rhythm, and the saxophone player joined in adding a touch of romance to the quiet atmosphere. She knocked back the last of her drink when she noticed the bottle of Vodka behind the counter. "Hey, Mike!" she said, holding it up.

He turned, and said, "It's yours. Congrats on the job!"

"Thank you. Tell Carmen hello," she said as she slipped a couple of ten bills under her glass.

No sooner than she got to the door, two guys bolted in causing her to stumble backward. One of the two cared less and had a seat at the bar. And the other one, Ricky Carlyle, stopped and said, "Hope you have a good time." She returned a hard glare. "You're holding a bottle of vodka." He returned her glare with a sarcastic grin. "Maybe we will run into each other again."

In the meantime, Detective Leary sat in his car scouting the area for leads to help him with his investigation. Over the last four month, eight deaths were caused by overdosing on heroin. "No thanks to the low price of heroin," he muttered.

He knew some of the bars on the south side were dark and catered to rough crowds. Even though most of them was located a little further south, Mike's Pub seemed to be a good place to start.

Several minutes later, he lit a cigarette and got out of his car. As he neared the entrance, the door swung open, and Renee rushed out.

"You come here often?" he asked as she whizzed by him.

She stopped and said, "Excuse me?"

"Be careful wherever you're headed to." She then realized it was Detective Leary. "The fog is thick tonight."

She shrugged her shoulders. "Not unusual."

"Did you happen to notice the two guys that entered the bar right before you walked out?"

"Yes. And no, I've never seen them before. You might want to use less gel on your hair. It's messing with your thinking."

He eyed the bottle of vodka in that she was carrying. "You might want to bag that."

"I don't think anybody around here will care about it. It's a good weapon, though."

He cracked a smile and said, "Enjoy your night."

When he turned to go inside the bar, she asked, "Detective? Didn't Serelley tell you who his accomplice was? I mean, your info came from him."

"No. No name or description. No matter my effort, he wasn't about to rat out the person. I can't say too much, but Maly and I are following another case that may lead us to this other person. If you happen to think of something, please call me no matter what hour it is." And he went inside the pub.

The dense fog caused for a slow walk home which gave her time to think about his answer. "The man knows more than he is letting on," she muttered.

Moments later she turned onto Ocean View Drive, and sudden fear rampaged through her body upon seeing a white car parked across the street.

What if that car belongs to one of the two guys that came into the bar? Maybe they were the ones that tried to run over me that one morning, she thought as she continued walking home.

"That's some crazy thinking, and I don't even use gel in my hair," she mumbled, and she shut her apartment door behind her.

Chapter Four

Deep sleep and vodka paved a perfect playground for nightmares. A dark blend of that horrid day two years ago, and what Detective Leary and Sargent Maly had told her, kept her paralyzed until late morning.

Suddenly, she snapped out of her deep sleep. "That's not my husband. That's not my husband," she cried.

She slumbered her way to the sofa and swallowed a couple of Vicodin. But no sooner than it hit her stomach, something didn't feel right, and she made a mad dash to the bathroom and threw up last night's spoiled indulgence.

"I don't need to be drinking, anymore," she muttered while splashing cool water on her face.

Moments later, she flipped through the TV channels and stopped on the local Christian network. The same lady preacher was on as the last time she watched this station. The sermon was about hope, again. Only this time she felt a sense of comfort embrace her while she listened to every word the lady said.

"If this feeling is real, then maybe it means my life will get better, and that God has something good waiting for me," she mumbled. "But right now, I need to call my doctor back home for a referral to a pain specialist."

Later that same morning, her doctor's office called back telling her to be at Dr. Jo Lunki's office located at Bay Side Hospital by two p.m. They, also, let her know that they had worked her in and not to be late.

The following morning, she sat at the computer and sipped black coffee from her favorite purple mug while visiting favorite websites. On her third trip to the kitchen to refill her mug, her phone vibrated with a text from Jaylon.

"He's having guests over tonight. Just great." She groaned and then returned his text with a phone call.

"Are you on your way?" Jaylon asked upon answering.

"No. It's going to take me a bit to get ready. You do realize it's my day off?"

"Yes. Start getting ready. I'll pick you up in twenty minutes. Oh, and you need to wear something nice." And he hung up.

"Nice," she said, irked. "And, it's my day off."

Twenty minutes later, he parked in front of her apartment. She grabbed her duffle bag and rushed out the door.

"Wow. Your second time here," she said as she got inside his vehicle. "You could have sent a limo. A red one."

He grinned. "Next time."

As Jaylon drove, he noticed how she kept looking at her phone. "You should turn the volume up." She gave him a blank look. "By the way you are staring at your phone, I would say you're expecting a very important phone call."

"I had a doctor's appointment yesterday. He put a rush on the test's results and he said would call me if he got them back today."

"Everything ok?"

"Just routine stuff," she said, not wanting to discuss it.

He cleared his throat. "I thought maybe you had a boyfriend."

She shook her head no, and thought, Boyfriend? Nope.

Two hours later, she adorned the dining room table with the most exquisite crystal, china, and flatware she had ever seen. She picked up a plate and turned it over. "Dublin, Ireland," she mumbled. "The man has good taste."

"Yes, I do," he said.

She gasped and clutched the plate against her chest to keep from dropping it. "And you shouldn't sneak up behind someone like that."

"Everything looks great. The caterer should be here anytime," he said.

"That's my cue to get ready."

A half hour later, his guests had arrived, and Jaylon was getting impatient for Renee to come back downstairs. And just as he started up the stairs to get her, he stopped dead in his tracks and grinned, liking what he saw. The lady that always wore sweatpants and a baggy shirt was dressed in skinny black jeans, a sheer purple blouse over a black camisole, and black stilettos.

She stopped at the bottom of the stairs and gave a slight grin. "You ok?"

"Yeah. I was, um . . . Everyone is seated at the table."

Jaylon introduced her as she served their drinks. As she poured coffee into his cup, she noticed a purple china cup sitting on top of the place setting next to him. "Are you expecting someone else?"

"Yes. You." He took the tray from her hand, set it behind him, and then pulled the chair for her. "I saw it the other day in a storefront window. Since purple is your favorite color, I thought you would like it."

"It's beautiful. Thank you."

Everyone was well into their meal, discussing the idea of recording a new CD. And as she listened, she closed her eyes and smiled, inhaling a faint scent of Jaylon's cologne. But the moment burned to a crisp as the talk of touring got rather heated. Jaylon didn't want to tour anymore. He wanted to be with his family. Several course words and strong opinions was voiced, but Jaylon remained adamant with his decision.

Renee felt more than out of place as their discussion was none of her business. She cleared her throat, and said, "Would anyone like a refill of their drink?"

Nobody answered her.

"Ok. Jaylon, I am going to start cleaning the kitchen."

Later that evening as she was filling the dishwasher, a whiff of Jaylon's cologne aroused her senses again. She looked at him and smiled.

He grinned. "Hi. I really appreciate everything you have done tonight. It all went over well. Well, except for the talk about touring" He then wrapped his arms around her waist and gently kissed her lips. He wanted to kiss her again, but he held back the temptation and let go.

She watched him walk back to his guests, and when he turned the corner to the living room, she touched her lips, and smiled, feeling a sweet rush of ecstasy sweep through her.

The following morning, Dr. Lunki's office called. He explained that the lab results were normal, as well as the other tests. In fact, they were identical to the lab reports her doctor in New York had sent him. He then gave a few suggestions that might help her which included not exercising too hard, and to continue the pain meds as needed.

"I don't understand," she said, upset. "I was so hoping he would have found the source of this pain."

Chapter Five

The china cup sat on a shelf surrounded by precious treasures that belonged to her two children. Renee picked up the cup and smiled reminiscing about that night. The feel of his warm body pressing against hers and his soft, inviting kiss made her yearn for more, but she stopped right there. Getting close to someone scared her, knowing they could be taken away from her like Paul was.

She shook her head to rid the memories. "It's time to get out this apartment."

A warm breeze flowed in from the bay, tousling her hair. She pushed a few tresses back off her face while basking in this rare moment of feeling alive and free.

Several blocks up, she sauntered by the local book and DVD store and noticed a sign on the window announcing local activities. "The Shoreline Six Mile Run. It's the day after Thanksgiving," she muttered, feeling the adrenaline ignite. "It's been three years since my last race. Pain, or no pain, I'm doing this." And she went inside the store.

A few weeks had passed, and the effects of overtraining had set in. Renee washed downed a couple of Vicodin capsules with coffee and then settled on the sofa.

It wasn't long before total peace surrounded her. She loved the relaxed feeling of her body sinking into the soft cushion, but the sound of her phone vibrating on the coffee table interrupted the moment. Jaylon had sent her a text wanting to speak with her ASAP.

"A stop by Laurens Bakery comes first," she said to herself as she grabbed her keys and billfold.

And a half hour later, she stood at his front door holding a large coffee in each hand.

"Hi," he said upon opening the door. "Why didn't you just come on in?"

"Hands are full."

He took one of the cups, and she followed him to the living room.

"I'm going to be leaving for a three-month tour," he said.

"They got their way," she said with a slight chuckle.

"Yes, they did, except for the making of a new CD. I don't like last minute planning, but I'm sure it will all work out. I hope, anyway," he quipped. "The reason I asked you to come over is that I would like for you to stay here while I am gone. Besides, I don't like the idea of you staying alone at your place. I mean, without someone around for you. It would, also, give my parents a break from having to check in on everything here at the house."

"I suppose I can stay here. Sure."

"Great. I appreciate it. My kids have been living with my parents since the last few tours. I know it's hard for them to have to keep watch on my house and run my kids here, there, and yonder. Though, they wouldn't have it any other way."

"It's not a problem. Really."

"And one more thing, something I want to you to think about while I'm gone. There is a huge stone house in the country that my brother and I have always loved."

"Ok," she said, wondering where he was going with all this.

"We used to make bets on which one of us would be the first to make a bid on it if it was to go up for sale. So, the day it went on the market we took a tour of the house, placed a bid, and the owners accepted it."

"Just where are you going with this?"

"I want you to come with us. There will more work involved, which means more money, and you wouldn't have to drive to work. Besides, you know I hate the area where you live. You deserve a better place to live." He drank the last of his coffee. "But don't answer just yet. Think on it and let me know when the tour is over," he said excitedly.

Chapter Six

Two weeks later, Jaylon and the band boarded a private jet, California bound.

In the meantime, Renee didn't waste any time routing a new running course from Jaylon's house, around Bay Park, and back to his house. Only this time she was more cautious, especially since the incidence in the park. She kept more attuned to her surroundings than the tunes coming from her earbuds.

The following few months were all about training for the race. Every other day of running turned into an everyday event and resting on Saturdays. There were a few times she thought she had seen the same white car that tried to run over her several months back, but she figured she was just paranoid.

The tour was into its third month when Jaylon unexpectedly came home. He said he was expecting something important in the mail, and that he wanted to check on a few other things, as well. Renee knew that was an excuse because she was taking care of everything while he was gone.

Later that same night, they were talking in the living room, and he brought up the subject of his wife only to turn the conversation to Renee. "You don't talk very much, if any, about your family. Did you and your husband have children?"

His calm voice let her know that he cared and that he wasn't trying to pry into her personal life.

She told him about her two children, and then said, "It's been a long time." She hesitated, remembering how Jaylon hugged her that one night. "I don't know. I haven't been touched emotionally or physically for so long." And she stopped talking, thinking she had said too much.

"I know," he said. "I know what you mean. You love someone so deeply and then illness, tragedy, or whatever else, takes them from you. I haven't touched anyone since my wife died. Her death left me numb." He paused. "I guess we do have something in common."

"Yeah. Well, I need to finish up some things in the back room," she said, wanting to end the conversation. Death was the last thing she wanted in common with him.

Later that night as she was folding clothes in the laundry room, Jaylon came and stood in the doorway. She looked over at him, and he said, "Thanks for listening." And he went upstairs before she could reply.

When she finished, she took a long hot shower and then dressed in a long T-shirt. She couldn't get their conversation off her mind, and tonight he unveiled a little of himself. A very personal side. She touched her lips, feeling the warm kiss he gave her that one night, and suddenly she was about to do something that she would never think of doing.

Her bare feet sunk into the plush carpeting as she made her way down the hallway towards the small beam of light coming from his bedroom. Her heart raced nervous, unsure of her actions, and then she stopped. She couldn't just invite herself into Jaylon's room. This wasn't like her.

When she turned to go back to her room, Jaylon saw a small bit of her shadow, and said, "Come in."

She just stood there feeling the erratic thump in her chest. She pushed the door open, and he held out his hand inviting her to come over to him.

Early the next morning, Jaylon rushed about the house preparing to leave for San Francisco. He went back to his room for his duffle bag and took one last look at Renee before leaving.

She was sleeping so sound and still that he didn't want to wake her. Right then he heard a still small voice, saying, "Make me first, Jaylon." And suddenly, he had remorse about last night. In fact, he felt like had betrayed Leighanna. But as far as the still small voice, he and Leighanna attended church quite often, so he knew when God was speaking to him. But, he wasn't about to admit that the unsettling feeling was a conviction for sleeping with Renee, no matter his reason for doing so.

Several hours after he had left, she dressed in lightweight running pants and a T-shirt. She grabbed her running shoes and headed down to the kitchen where she saw a note lying on the table.

Renee,

You were sleeping so sound that I didn't want to wake you. I'll be in San Francisco today and through tomorrow night. I will call when I can. Jaylon

"Nothing," she muttered. "It was nothing to him. He came home for a one-night stand." She threw her shoes on the floor and slipped them on. "But then again, he came home to me when he could have any woman that he desired while on tour. Then again, he is not that way." She tied her shoelaces and rushed out the door.

The cool wind blew through her hair as she ran along the streets. But just as she reached Bay Park, everything that Leary had said about her family raced through her head. And, not only that, sleeping with Jaylon bothered her more than she wanted to admit. She circled the park and then headed south on West Bay Avenue to her apartment.

She slumped down on the sofa and rubbed her legs. The hard-aggravating pain let her know she had overdone it only this time it was to the point of unbearable.

She went to the kitchen to get a couple of Vicodin pills, but the bottle was empty. It was then she realized she had forgotten to call the doctor's office for a refill. Thanksgiving was a few days away, and her doctor was out of the office for the rest of the week. She knew there was probably a doctor on call, but she figured they wouldn't refill a narcotic pain reliever not knowing her medical situation, nor was she going to go to the ER. "What am I going to?" she mumbled, trying not to panic.

She went back to the living room, and her attention was drawn to a shelf where a plush doll and a gothic cross that belonged to her daughter Chloe, and a red train that belonged to her son Pauly, sat. She sighed hard and turned the TV on to drown out her thoughts, and the same lady preacher was on, again.

"First it was hope which I gave up on, and now it's peace. I don't see either one coming my way," Renee muttered. She then fluffed the pillow next to her and laid down.

A few hours later, she awoke to the evening news reporting about Christians being taken hostage by radical extremist groups. "Even the news doesn't give much hope. Not even for peace," she grumbled. She then grabbed her keys from the coffee table and left.

Mike's Pub neon sign glowed in the night sky, and every

few seconds it flickered like it was going to go out. She chuckled and went inside.

"What'll you have tonight, Miss Renee?" Mike asked, trying to be funny.

"Just a coke. So, is something going on here?" He looked at her not understanding what she meant. "Your neon light is acting nervous."

Mike chuckled and set the soda in front of her. "Nothing going on, but it is a good attention grabber. Help yourself to as many refills as your heart desires."

A few moments later, a couple of guys walked in. One was the same guy she had seen in here before, Ricky Carlyle. He sat across from her while the other guy went to the other end of the bar. Ricky studied her for a moment and then laughed to himself.

Mike set a beer in front of him. He knew by the quick shifting movements of Ricky's eyes at Renee that he was scouting her out.

"Leave her alone, Ricky. Do not make her one of your clients," Mike said adamantly.

"I don't make anyone a client. They have freedom of choice," Ricky quipped.

Renee overheard the two of them talking, and she darted a cold look at Ricky.

"Like I said, leave her alone," Mike said, and he went to the other end of the bar.

Ricky popped a few pretzels into his mouth. "She already is my client," he muttered to himself. "In a sorted way."

Renee reached over the bar to refill her glass with coke. And as she put the soda gun dispenser back in its holder, she sensed someone sitting down next to her. She sat her glass down and looked at him. His stone black eyes peered into hers like they were saying her name.

Right away Mike noticed that Ricky had moved over by Renee. Ricky held up his glass motioning for a refill. Mike came over and set another beer in front of him. He then gave Renee a direct glance. "I'll be back," he said her.

She knew right then that Ricky was a street pharmacist.

"He seems protective of you," Ricky said to her.

"He's a good friend."

"By the way, I'm Ricky. I have seen you in here a few times, and I have seen you out running."

"Do you have a special field of interest?" she asked. He gave her a blank look. "Um, how do I put this. You are in the business of helping people live the high life."

"That's one way to put it," he said with a smirk on his face. "Sometimes a little extra zing makes life livelier. Skies the limit. Though some have reached beyond the sky and they didn't come back. Sucks." He chuckled and said, "For me anyway." He downed the last of his beer. "Nice talking. Maybe we will meet again." He laid money on the bar and lit a cigarette on his way out the door.

Ok, she thought. I've got nothing to lose. Maybe this Ricky guy can get me through the weekend. Maybe I can get something stronger. Vicodin doesn't always do the trick.

"See you later, Mike," she said, slipping a ten bill under her glass. And she left.

Fog hovered the streets as she looked for Ricky. And just as she turned the corner, she gasped and stopped dead in her tracks. Ricky had appeared out of nowhere.

"Ha! Scare ya? Surprise," Ricky said, grinning.

"You know that I overheard you and Mike talking, so let's skip the chit-chat," she said, with slight New York accent. "My doc is out of town, and I need something to get me through the weekend. Something stronger than Vicodin."

Most of his clients talk the talk, but not her. No street lingo, just straightforward and blunt. He liked that.

He blew cigarette smoke into the air, took one last hard drag, and threw it on the ground. "Huh. That New York accent must only come out when you're mad. Or nervous." He cleared his throat. "Ok. I'll be on the pier near Washington Avenue. I would do business here, but there's talk of a cop nosing around. You got thirty minutes to get there."

Chapter Seven

Ricky leaned against the railing along the boardwalk. He looked at his watch every few seconds when the sound of a bottle breaking over by the bar startled him. He jerked around only to see Renee walking toward him. A slight smile came across his face, and he calmed down.

Without speaking, he led her to the edge of the pier. He reached inside his leather jacket and pulled out a small red box. "This should do the trick. Dilaudids. The real thing. All your troubles and pain will vanish. And this time, your first time, is on me. And, um, I wouldn't take these before going for a run, or doing anything. Just saying, though."

"A red box and on you," she said, ignoring his comment about running. "And the real thing, eh."

A smirk came across his face. "The real thing? How would you know otherwise?"

"Didn't mean to crease the leather," she said. "My doctor back home prescribed these when I was in the hospital. Plus, I knew a few tweekers that banged heroin, and Dilaudids,

35

OxyContin, and the like, were their back-up. I never gave any thought to using, though.

He laughed under his breath, and said, "My sweet Renee, I would never give you anything tainted. I have to keep a good reputation, or my filthy rich clients would stop buying from me. I'll catch you later." And he left.

When she arrived back at her apartment, she set the box on the coffee table, got a coke from the fridge, and then opened the red box. Just as she started to pop one of the pills in her mouth, she stopped and looked at the cross and train on the shelf. "Everything I had was ripped away from me," she mumbled, and she swallowed both pills with the coke.

She turned the TV on and waited for some mental relief, and relief from the pain in her legs.

Twenty minutes went by and nothing. And then all at once, she was surrounded by total peace. Every ounce of her body and state of mind relaxed, and a slight smile came across her face. She didn't want this moment to end. And from that moment on, Ricky's phone number was at the top of her contacts list.

Chapter Eight

Ten weeks later Jaylon came home. He dropped his bags on the kitchen floor and headed upstairs. Upon reaching the last step, Renee bumped into him as she was heading down.

"Hi. I thought I heard the kitchen door slam. It's good to have you home."

He embraced her, and said, "I'm glad to be home, too." The feeling of her warms hands against his back made him glad to be home even more. "I'm taking a shower. I'll be down later."

As he walked away, he turned and grinned at her.

"What?" she asked.

"You just called my home, home. As in your home."

She smiled and said nothing as he closed his bedroom door. But, the way he hugged her brought back memories of their night together, of which neither one had talked about since.

A few weeks later, Renee walked toward Queens Way warming up for an evening run. A slight wind kicked in rustling the leaves on the street, and the evening clouds spit out the first flakes of snow. Even though she loved the winter season, she wasn't quite ready for it to arrive. With a quick change of mind, she headed for her car and drove to Mikes. Good 'ol Mike's Pub on the bad side of town. According to Jaylon, that is, she thought.

She pulled up along the curb in front of the pub and noticed a white car parked up the street. "Ricky," she muttered.

She sat in her usual spot at the bar and listened to the saxophone player lay down a soothing tune.

"Hey there. Where ya been? Everything ok?" Mike asked all in one breath.

"Yeah. Just busy moving. A coke please."

"Where did you move to," he asked as he set a coke in front of her. "I hope to a nicer area than where you were living. You deserve better."

"So, I've heard. My boss's house. He is buying a huge home in the country for him and his family, so he thought it would be a good idea for me to live there and work. He paid my lease off and put my things in storage. More money, too."

Mike sort of chuckled. "As long as you have your free time and all. Hey, just some FYI here. Ricky has been coming by more than usual. He is nice, but at the same time, he is bad news.

"Thanks. I'll keep my eyes open."

Someone at the other end of the bar hollered for Mike. "Guess that's my cue. I'll talk to you in a bit."

The soothing song ended, and the band turned up the mood by playing a lively rhythm. And just in time for Ricky to walk in and slide onto the barstool beside her.

"Maybe you should find another place to sit. Mike seems to think we have become friends if you know what I mean," she said.

"Yeah? Well, that's his problem. Let's dance." He grabbed her hand and led her onto the dance floor. "You know how to do this." He made a quick turn and stopped. She wasn't dancing. "What's wrong?"

"I know how to do this? How would you know that?" she asked, irked. She had never told him anything about her life.

"Don't be so defensive. I'm not that bad of a guy," he said as he began to lead her to a fast swing.

When the beat slowed, he brought her up close to him, and his black eyes peered into hers. She stopped dancing and took a few steps back. "Let's go sit down," she said. She didn't like him standing that close to her, or how his eyes peered into her eyes like they were saying her name.

"I'm going outside and have a smoke," he said.

She took a drink of her coke and watched him leave while trying to shake off the fact that he knew something about her.

"Saw you dancing with him," Mike said, interrupting her thoughts. He wiped the bar off and then refilled her drink. "I'll give him credit on the account that he can dance, and you're not so bad yourself. But watch your step with him. You just may be swinging with the devil."

Renee smiled. "Maybe. But I can't turn down a good swinger."

Mike laughed.

"I need to be going. Tell Carmen hello." She needed to find Ricky is what she really meant.

The only light near the pub was in the side parking lot where Ricky was leaning against a red sports car. He took several long drags of his cigarette when he saw her approaching him. The way she walked turned him on, but her cold hard glare is what sent him over the edge. "But she sure can dance," he muttered.

She didn't have to say anything to him for him to know what she was after.

"Wait a few seconds after I leave, before following me.

Turn right at the stop sign, go a few blocks, and then turn left. You'll see my car ahead of you," he said.

She understood and did as he instructed. She then followed him from a distance to an apartment complex located a few blocks south of where she used to live. She parked beside his car and rolled her window down.

"Wanna come inside?" he asked as he walked over to her.

"No," she said, holding a twenty bill between her fingers. "I thought you had a white car."

He looked at her for a moment and gave a slight grin. "But red cars are your favorite."

She ignored his comment.

"Anyway, I don't have the Dilaudids right now, but this is better," he said, holding a small bundle of foil, that was taped up beyond ridiculous, between his fingers. "Five milligrams of black tar, heroin, dope, smack, or whatever you choose to call it. And, um, there is a pharmacy just a block south of the bay where you can get syringes without a prescription. That is if you plan on banging it. Just saying, though. Keep your money."

"I'll check it out. Thanks for the info." She snatched the bundle from his fingers and shoved the money at him. "I'll call you. If there is a next time." And she drove away before he could say anything else.

"Oh, my sweet Renee, there will be a next time." He grinned and said, "You can bet your life your life on that."

"He might as well be the devil," she muttered. She drove around the last curve of Queens Shores Drive and sighed a bit of relief seeing that Jaylon's vehicle wasn't in the driveway.

I should have kept my apartment she thought as she hurried upstairs to her room. She locked the door and begun what she had never thought of doing, let alone use a vein in her foot so there wouldn't be any track marks on her arms.

Early afternoon the next day, Jaylon knocked on her bedroom door. Instinct told him something was wrong because she had never slept past eleven a.m. After several attempts and no reply, he pounded on the door. "Renee! Are you all right?" He waited a few seconds, and then went inside.

She was still. Dead still. Jaylon put his hand in front of her nose to see if she was breathing, but he couldn't feel her breath. He shook her shoulder. Nothing. He shook her shoulder, again. Still nothing. He sat down beside her trying not to panic. And then, she snapped awake and gasped, startling him.

"What's going on?" she asked, confused.

"You've been asleep all morning, and now it's afternoon. I was just making sure you were ok."

"I'm fine. I took a new pain medicine last night. I'll be down shortly."

"Are you sure you're ok?"

"Yes. I'm fine."

"Ok, then." He turned toward the bathroom to leave, and then he looked back at her.

"I'll be down soon," she said, and he went downstairs.

She stumbled to the bathroom, and her foot hit the syringe causing it to slide across the floor and slam against the bathtub. She picked it up and started to throw it across the room, but ramped cold chills ran through her, and she spewed her guts into the toilet.

Moments later, she splashed cold water on her face, and then she felt a sharp throb on the top of her left foot. There were a slight bruise and a streak of dried blood from where she had injected the small amount of dope. And next to her, laying on the counter was a small chunk of dope that she had cut in half. She wrapped the dope in the same foil and tape that it came in, along with the syringe, and then threw it in one of the bathroom vanity drawers.

"You are not going to let yourself get hooked on this junk, nor are you going let Jaylon see you hung over ever again," she said to herself as she got into the shower.

Afterward, she went downstairs. The scent of winter pine reminded her that Christmas was only a few weeks away. Decorations were lying on the dining room table and the floor. And strings of lights were bunched up at the bottom of the front door, along with a wreath.

"Hey there," Jaylon said. "It's about time you came down. I am volunteering you to help me, instead of you doing your usual job," he said, climbing up a latter.

Renee yawned. "Oh, really?"

"You're still tired after all that sleeping? So, what kind of medicine are you taking?" he asked as he put the last section of the tree up. "We should have bought a real tree."

"We?" she said, confused. "Jaylon, that is something I have wanted to talk about-"

"I'm just concerned about you," he said, not paying attention to what she had just said. "Anyway. I have not put up a Christmas tree in several years. My mom goes way out on the decorating, so I figure why bother putting up mine when I am going to be at mom and dad's house."

"Why this year?" she asked, yawning. "Is something special going on?"

"Well, you're here," he said.

She frowned. "I'm going to fix some coffee."

A pot of coffee and three hours later, they was finished.

"The house looks pretty darn awesome, but I'm starving. Let's go eat," he said.

He drove north of the city, and asked, "What sounds good to you?"

"I love Italian food," she said, grinning.

"There is an authentic Italian restaurant that I go to on

occasion, and believe me, you won't get any better Italian cuisine this side of Italy."

Twenty minutes later they arrived at the restaurant, and a waiter greeted them as they walked inside. "Hello, Jaylon. Your usual dining area is free tonight."

"Perfect. Thank you."

They followed him to a private room where dark red fabrics and dim lighting cast a romantic mood.

"Wow. This is nice," Renee said.

Jayon smiled. "I knew you would like it."

They dined on the fine cuisine until their stomachs were full.

Renee gave a slight laugh, and said, "The food was delizioso. Thank you."

"You're welcome. The place never fails when it comes to fine dining." He then took her hand and said a short prayer thanking God for their friendship and their time together tonight.

The waiter came by and set a black check holder on the table. Jaylon put his credit card and several hundred-dollar bills inside it and handed it back to the waiter. Jaylon noticed her wide-eyed look. "One of the perks of being a rock star."

She laughed. He couldn't help but laugh, too. He never flaunted the fact that he was a millionaire, nor did he have the egotistical attitude that tends to go with fame.

The waiter returned with Jaylon's credit card and thanked him for being so generous.

"You have always treated my company and me more than well. Merry Christmas," Jaylon said to him. He then turned his attention back to Renee. "Let's get out of here. I want to take you to a special place."

Jaylon held Renee's hand tightly as he drove out of the city and on through the snow-covered countryside. The further he drove the deeper the snow got making it hard to drive.

"Finally," he said, turning onto another road. He let go of her hand and held the wheel with both hands. "I hope I can make it up the hill. I was so excited to come here that I didn't give any thought as to how bad the roads might be out here."

After a slow climb up the hill, he shifted into park, and they got out.

"Look down there, in the valley."

"This is amazing," she said. "Never in my life have I seen a Christmas scene like this. It reminds me of my favorite artist paintings where everything is so detailed."

"I used to bring my wife and kids here every year. It was such a special time for us," he said, with a gleam in his eyes.

"Don't ever let those memories go," she said.

He smiled and held her close to him. "Never."

When they arrived home, Jaylon turned the Christmas lights on while she fixed two mugs of hot chocolate.

"You know, I don't think I have seen you smile as much as you have tonight. I'm glad you enjoyed it," he said, putting a movie into the DVD player.

"Actually, I was thinking the same thing about you. This was good for both of us. I won't forget it," she said, setting the mugs of hot chocolate on the coffee table. "But, I have been wondering about something. You have never talked about—"

"I have to be honest," he interrupted, thinking he knew what she was going to say. "I enjoyed that night we shared, but at the same time, I felt like I betrayed Leighanna. She was the only lady I had ever been with, and I never once gave a thought of cheating on her. Even the back-stage passes didn't tempt me. I despise women like that, anyway. Leighanna was my world. This may sound stupid, but I don't think God —"

"Jaylon, I was asking about your brother. You mentioned him when you told me about buying the house and—"

"I think the world of you. There's not a morning that I wake up not thinking about you. I'm just not ready for any kind of relationship."

"It's ok. I understand," she said just to keep him from saying any more.

He may never get over Leighanna's death, but she now regrets walking down the hallway that one night.

"Now, to change the subject. Would you go with me to my parent's house for Christmas? They really want to meet you, and so do my kids. You will love grandma. She is one of the most loving and giving people I know."

"That is your family. I wouldn't want them to think that we are a couple. Or in love."

"I know you'll have a good time. Besides, Christmas isn't just for family, it's for sharing with friends, too."

"Friends," she said, with a slight laugh. And now, she didn't want to be around him. "I'm going to bed now."

The excitement of the night dwindled. He knew by her turn of mood and short words that she was upset which made him upset with himself.

"We can watch the movie another time. I'll turn the lights off," he said as she left the room.

Renee sat on the bathroom floor watching her blood seep from the needle and onto her foot. She loved how heroin took her thoughts about the past, and now the present, away. Plus, if what Detective Leary had told was true, she wondered what else her husband had kept from her, let alone all the lies.

"I was so blind to it all. I should have seen it," she mumbled. "And now, Jaylon is messing with my emotions just to help himself, or so it seems."

Chapter Nine
One Week Later

Renee decided to go with Jaylon to his parent's house for Christmas, and he was more than anxious to get there. In fact, he was like a little kid who couldn't wait for Christmas morning to arrive.

"Wake up sleepy head. It's Christmas Eve," Jaylon said, standing beside her bed. "Are you still going with me?"

Even though her joints ached just enough to make her change her mind, there was no way she was going to disappoint him. She threw the covers over her head, and mumbled, "I'll be down shortly."

"Great," he said, excited.

When he left, she opened the nightstand drawer, popped open the bottle of Dilaudid's and cut one in half all the while knowing a little jolt of her bitter friend would be more satisfying. But she had never been high around Jaylon, and she wasn't going to take a chance of nodding off in front of him and his family.

A half hour later, he heard her say, "Ok. Let's go."

"Took you long enough," he said, teasing her.

It had snowed all morning, and there was no sign of it stopping. Jaylon wanted to arrive at his parent's house by noon, but whiteout conditions caused them to arrive an hour later.

"We made it," he said, pulling into their driveway.

Their home was cozy warm, and a scent of apples and cinnamon graced the air. He snuggled her hand into his and led her to a room where the sound of laughter came from.

"Merry Christmas, everyone," he said. "This is Renee."

His dad muted the sound on the TV, stood up, and shook her hand. "I'm Dave. It's nice to meet you."

Jaylon then introduced his son Dyllon, his daughter Reighanna, and their pastor Benny Lorens.

Renee gave a shy hello as Jaylon whisked her to the kitchen.

"Mom, grandma," he said. They were busy preparing the food that they didn't hear him. "Mom," he said, louder.

"Jaylon, you don't have to ask permission to taste the food," she said. When he didn't respond, she gave him a sharp glance.

"This is Renee."

"Oh, my. I'm sorry. I am so glad you're here," she said, hugging her. "Just make yourself at home, honey. There is no reason to feel shy or out of place here."

"I've been after Jaylon to bring you over, so we could meet you," his grandma said.

Jaylon laughed at their excitement. "Just relax. Your family here," he said to Renee, and he went back to the family room.

Family, Renee thought, missing her children.

"Is there something I can help with?" she asked them.

"Um, not right now, but I heard that you love to bake," his

mom said.

Renee looked her confused.

She grinned, and said, "I was there when Jaylon interviewed you for the job."

"Oh, that's right. I had forgotten about that."

"By the way, my name is Natalie, and this is Dave's mom, Arlene."

Arlene laughed. "Sweetie just call me grandma. I'm not sure how I would act if anyone here called me by my name."

"Ok, grandma it is," Renee said.

Later that evening, they sat around the dining room table that was graced with a gorgeous Christmas setting, and carols softly played in the background. She relaxed and listened to the different conversations while enjoying every mouth savoring bite of the meal.

"So, what do you think?" Jaylon asked her amongst the conversations.

"Good thing I didn't stay home. I would have missed out on a lot, especially the food."

Reighanna, who was sitting across the table from them, noticed how her dad liked Renee, and if not, love her. There was a spark in his eyes that she hadn't seen since her mom died. And then she realized who Renee was and halted all conversations, saying, "I have several videos of the dance company you were in."

"Dance videos?" Renee said, looking at her and then at Jaylon.

He returned a blank look, and then said, "Oh! That is where I have seen you before. My band was going to shoot a music video, and we were looking for a certain style of dance. It was supposed to be something totally different from we had done before. So, our manager obtained several videos of dance companies, and one of them happened to be yours. But personal issues within the band happened and it got pushed aside, indefinitely."

"Oh," was all Renee could think to say.

"And, since Reighanna is quite the dancer, I gave her the videos."

"Oh," she said, again.

Dyllon sensed that Renee felt awkward and decided to interrupt. "Dad, you should have recorded a Christmas album," he said, with sarcasm in his voice. "You know, keep it your grungy hard rock music."

"Uh . . . No," Jaylon snapped.

Thank you Dyllon, Renee thought, and she continued enjoying the meal.

Later that evening, after the roads had been plowed, they went for a drive northbound. Reighanna had a huge grin on her face. She knew where they were going.

When Jaylon got top of the hill, he shifted into park, and they got out of the Escalade. A mesmerizing hush came over them as they gazed at the shimmering scenery in the valley below.

Tears streaked down the sides of Reighanna's face. "Mom is here with us dad. I can feel her grinning with pure joy."

Dyllon swallowed hard and smiled.

"I remember the last time we were here," Jaylon said in a hushed tone. "It was the coldest December. Record cold, at that. Leighanna was all bundled up, shivering like crazy, and yet she was so happy that the cold didn't faze her."

Natalie walked over and hugged him. "She is still with us."

The closeness of his family and the love they have for each other made Renee miss her children that much more. This was way too much for her to grasp and the thought of bolting down the hill to get away tempted her.

Dyllon walked over to her, and said, "I'm glad you're

here."

"Thank you," Renee said.

Moments later, they piled back into the Escalade and headed to Jaylon's house.

When they pulled into his driveway, he held Renee's hand, and said, "Thank you."

Reighanna knew right then that her dad loved Renee. This was the first time he had shown feelings of affection toward another lady since the death of her mother.

Once they got inside the house, and with a flip of the light switch, the living room, and dining room, glistened.

"Everything is beautiful, especially the tree," Natalie said.

"I had help decorating," Jaylon said.

Natalie glanced over at Renee with appreciation.

Good grief, Renee thought. Surely, she isn't thinking that Jaylon and I are a couple. She then went to the kitchen for some space.

As she got a bottle of water from the fridge, she heard, "Jaylon usually stays the night with us on Christmas Eve. Why don't you stay, as well?"

She turned and saw grandma standing in the doorway.

"You shouldn't be alone on this special night. You have done so much for us."

What in the world have I done for them, she thought.

Jaylon came into the kitchen and saw the frustrated look on Renee's face. "Come upstairs with me." And he led her to her room.

He wiped her tears away with the back of his hand. "I know tonight was hard for you."

"You and your grandma keep saying I have done something special, but I haven't," she said, upset. "Please, just go back to your family. I'll be down in a few minutes."

He looked into her eyes and saw the hurt he had caused

her. "I'm sorry if I've hurt you or caused confusion."

I don't know what you are talking about." She lied. "Just go be with your family."

After he left, she locked the door and then opened the nightstand drawer. "I have to stay clear-minded tonight," she said to herself. She slammed the drawer shut. She opened it, again, and slammed it shut. "Augh! Stop. This is insane. Go downstairs."

When she turned to leave, she caught a glimpse of herself in the bathroom mirror. She wasn't sure if she knew who the person was that was looking back at her, anymore. Too many lies, and so much taken from me, and now tonight, she thought. She grabbed the Dilaudids and syringe from the drawer and put them in her makeup bag.

When they returned to his parent's house, they sat around the tree laughing and talking late into the night when a hot sweat came over her.

"I'm sorry everyone, but I really need to go to bed," she said.

Jaylon sort of frowned at her as they told her good night. He thought it was a bit strange for her to be turning in so soon. When he heard the guest's bedroom door shut, he said a silent prayer of protection over her.

"Never would I have thought I'd be shooting pills into a vein on my foot just to keep from having withdrawals," she muttered, sitting on the edge of the bed. But she couldn't do it, not in his parent's house. It was bad enough she had taken dope into Jaylon's house. So, she changed her mind and swallowed the pill.

Afterward, as she lay in bed, she thought about how there was so much love between them, and they had passed their love onto her by making her feel like she was a part of them. Maybe that is what grandma and Jaylon meant, she thought.

Just by being with them, I helped them heal some of their wounds from the past.

Her thoughts then roamed to Jaylon's kids. Reighanna, with her long dark hair and big brown eyes, had to resemble her mother. She had never seen a photo of her mother, but by judging Reighanna's looks, she must have been stunning. And Dyllon was the spitting image of his dad. And now, even more so, she wondered what Jaylon's brother looked like.

In the midst of her thoughts, and the sound of laughter coming from the living room, she drifted off to sleep.

Chapter Ten

Jaylon sat on the sofa with his feet propped on the coffee table, listening to messages on the house phone. A few friends had invited him to a New Year's Eve party, but he wasn't interested. He turned the ringer off and turned on the TV.

A few moments later, Renee plopped down beside him. "What ya watching?" she asked, trying to be funny.

"I believe this is called the noon news," he said, with a smirk on his face. "It's one of those shows where they talk about stuff in our neck of the woods, including the ton of snow that we are getting over the next few days. So much for New Years. Not that I planned on doing anything, anyway."

Renee started to reply, but her attention was redirected to a breaking news flash about a drug cartel in the area, and Detective Leary was being interviewed. He told the investigative reporter that he and Sargent Maly were looking into the situation.

"You seem really interested in that report," Jaylon said.

"Drug Cartel? Just because there are drugs on the streets

doesn't mean there's a cartel."

"Dealers get them from somewhere. But with Maly in on it, as well, I'm sure they will solve it."

"You say that as if you know him."

"I've known him for a while."

That's nice, she thought. "On that note, I'm going out."

"You might wanna keep an eye on the weather," she heard him say as she headed out the kitchen door. "The snow will arrive tonight and may have blizzard like effects."

"I will see you later." And she left.

"Drug Cartel. Why did that spark her interest? She doesn't use drugs," he muttered. "And she knows that detective, too."

Renee pressed Ricky's name on her phone's speed dial menu as she drove south on West Bay Avenue.

On the fourth ring, Ricky answered. "Make it quick, my sweet."

"I need to meet you tonight."

Ricky told her to meet him at a bar on the south-west side.

Twenty minutes later, she parked near the entrance of the bar, and at the same time, another car parked at the end of the same block. It was the same white car that she had seen before. The two guys in the car didn't get out, but she did notice how they were staring at her with intent.

Further up the street Detective Leary and Sargent Maly sat in an unmarked police car scouting the area for a local drug dealer, when Detective Leary said, "Is that who I think it is going inside?" He picked up his binoculars and adjusted the strength to get a closer look. "Renee MacKie. Huh."

"What?" Sargent Maly said. "What about her."

"Nothing." Detective Leary said. He wasn't going to say what his thoughts were, because he didn't want to make accusations before he had proof.

Maly then received a text, and he texted back, *"No. Not this time. I'm with Leary. Stay put."*

Ricky sat slouching in a booth near the back, and he had company. He eyed her as she approached him. He loved how she walked without a care in the world, but her cold hard glare is what turned him on. He gave her a slight smile as she sat down.

"What can I get you," a waitress asked her.

"Just a coke, please," Renee said.

"I'll be right back," the waitress said.

Renee glared at his friend. She didn't like the idea he had someone with him. For all she knew, he could be an undercover cop.

"Ever think of diving into something different, like . . . cocaine, or as I call it, devil's dust?" Ricky asked. "Add it to heroin, and you'll be riding high and land with ease. You'll be back for more my little lady."

The waitress returned, set her coke on the table, and left.

Renee downed it. "I'm going to get another one. I'll be back."

Ricky gave a smug laugh. He knew it wouldn't be long before she would be running to him for more, and he liked the idea of getting her under his control.

"Fine look'n lady you have," his friend said. Ricky frowned. "For a client that is."

A few minutes later, Renee came back, and said, "Ok. Just what I came for. I'm not ready to dance with the devil." They made their swap, but he wouldn't keep her money. "Take it! You don't give for free."

He crossed his arms on the table, leaned forward, and whispered, "For you I do."

His friend chuckled.

"Who's your friend?" she asked, point blank.

"Friend," Ricky said. Seeing she wasn't amused, he said, "Phil."

"By the way, you can call your other friends off. I don't need to be followed."

"Excuse me?" he snapped. "Whatever are you talking about?"

"There's two men sitting in a car not far from mine. They were staring at me and all. I swore they were going to jump me," she said, with a New York accent.

"There's that accent, again." He cleared his throat. "And you just assume that I have something to do with them? Oh, believe me, if I wanted you followed my guys wouldn't be visible to you. I'm not that careless. Chill the talk my sweet. Nobody is gonna mess with ya. I'll make sure of that."

She shot him a hard glare and left.

The moment she walked out, she looked up the street, but the car wasn't there. The idea that they could be cops went through her mind, but she doubted that. They had no reason to follow her.

"Maybe I should change running courses," she muttered, getting into her car. "Wait, I haven't been running in a while." She sighed hard, knowing she had missed The Shore Line Race. Ricky was right about one thing, she thought, Dilaudids and running do not mix.

By the time she drove onto the main road, the snow was blowing hard causing near white-out conditions. She looked in the rear-view mirror, making sure she didn't pull out in front of another car only to see the white car tailing her. And as it passed by, it veered toward her front bumper, causing her to swerve off the road, and back on.

"God, get me home," she said out loud. She gripped the wheel to keep from losing control of her car. And ten minutes later, the Queens Shores Drive street sign came into view.

Chapter Eleven

The following week, Renee head music blaring from the living room which made for a perfect time to leave without him knowing. She didn't want him seeing her in the hung-over state she was in. But no sooner than her hand touched the kitchen doorknob, the music grew quiet.

"Going out?" Jaylon asked as he walked into the kitchen.

She snapped around. "Looks that way. Why?"

"Just wondering. We have not crossed paths in several days" Besides the edgy attitude, he knew something was off with her, and she looked hung over. "Are you ok? You look pale and exhausted."

"We are out of a few cleaning supplies," she said, just to keep him from asking anything else.

"Well, anyway. I owe you an apology. I got so caught up in the excitement of the holidays that I forgot to give you your Christmas present."

"That makes us even."

He handed her an envelope with a red and purple ribbon

tied around it.

"Pretty," she said, smiling. And as she pulled the card out, several hundred-dollar bills slipped out and landed on the floor, and she quickly picked them up. "I, um . . . Do you know how much this is?"

"Well, yeah," he laughed. "I am the one that put the money in it."

"Jaylon, the gift I got you doesn't even come close to this."

"You have given me more than you will ever know," he said. "You deserve it. So, go buy yourself something really special."

She hugged him, and said, "Thank you. I'll take this to my room."

She carelessly put the envelope in the top dresser drawer and closed it leaving a piece of the red ribbon dangling outside of it. She then searched her closet for the James Bond movie she had purchased a while back at the bookstore knowing he wanted it to add to his collection. "Here it is," she said. She took it to his room and laid it on his bed.

"I'll order a pizza tonight and rent a movie," he said as she came downstairs. "What do you think of the music?"

She shrugged her shoulders. "Sounds a little like your music."

"Since you like my music, I'll take that as a compliment."

"Bye," she said, grinning.

"God, please watch over her. Just. . . watch over her," he prayed.

A half hour later, she sat a bench in Bay Park watching the ocean waves crash onto the shore. I can buy a lot of special things with that money, she thought. Not every day is a thousand dollars handed to you, especially from your favorite rock star. She laughed and then muttered, "He is very special."

Amidst her muttering, she felt a cold leather glove touch

the back of her neck. She gasped, nearly jumping out of her skin.

"Relax. It's just me," Ricky said. He then handed her a small deli sack that contained an open bag of chips and a sub sandwich. "Just for you, my sweet."

"Got hungry on the way here, did ya?" she joked. "I'd stay and chat, but I have places to go, and my boss is bringing supper home tonight."

"It's not good to keep a man waiting," he said, with a smirk on his face.

"See you later."

"Later." He looked out at the bay, and muttered, "Yes, you will, my sweet Renee. Yes, you will."

When she returned home, she set the shopping bags on the counter and noticed a note by the stove.

Renee,

I am at mom and dad's and will return later this evening. I'll order the pizza, and we can watch the movie you got me. Thank you! I needed it to finish my James Bond collection. Jaylon

In the meantime, Jaylon sat at the kitchen table talking with his mom and dad while waiting for his kids to come home from school.

Natalie, his mom, set a turkey sandwich and a mug of coffee in front of him. "What's wrong? You're rather quiet which means something is occupying your mind."

He wanted to tell them about Renee, but he didn't want to betray her trust, nor did he want to talk out of speculation.

He took a sip of coffee and thought for a moment. "I gotta be careful how I say this, but I'm worried about Renee. She may be into something that could end badly, even tragic," he said. "At the same time, I hope I'm wrong and just being paranoid."

"Can you tell us what the problem is?" his dad asked.

Jaylon nodded his head no and wiped his hand on a napkin. "She doesn't tell anyone my business, and I don't tell anyone hers. And if you would, call Benny and have him pray for her."

Just then, Reighanna be-bopped through the door.

"Hey, sweetheart," Jaylon said.

"Hi," she said, giving him a big bear hug. "Will you drop me off at school on your way home? There's a basketball game tonight. And I need a ride back, too."

"Anything for you."

Moments later, Dyllon and his girlfriend, Tyler, came in. "Hey, dad. Grandma, we are famished. The school's lunch was not fit to eat."

As Natalie fixed them a sandwich, they laughed at Dyllon's humorous talk about things that happened at school. Tyler chimed in and said that those things could only happen to Dyllon.

Jaylon chuckled at Dyllon. "Just as long as the principal doesn't call me saying that your grades have fallen off the record.

"It's all good," Dyllon said.

"Are you staying for supper, Jaylon?" Natalie asked.

He looked at his watch. "No. It's almost five. I left a note for Renee telling her I would bring home a pizza." Natalie tried not to smile, but he knew that look on her face. "And no mom, we are not a couple. Oh, by the way, you know the house that Kohl and I have been wanting? We are buying it, and in the next few months we will be moving in."

"That house is plenty big. It could hold several families, and they still wouldn't be in each other's way," Dave said, chuckling.

"So, you're done with touring?" Dyllon asked.

"Yes," Jaylon replied, excited.

Reighanna hugged him. "I can't wait. We will all be together from now on."

"I can't wait, either. Let's get a move on. Love you guys" he said as he and Reighanna walked out the door.

He dropped Reighanna off at school and then called Renee. "Hi there. So, what do you think about tonight? Should I go ahead and order a pizza?"

"Sure. I guess."

"Great. See you in a bit. Oh, one more thing, I have to pick up Reighanna after the basketball game at school and take her back to mom and dad's house."

"No problem," she said, feeling the cold sweat of withdrawal wash over her.

No sooner than they hung up, a text from Ricky came through that read, *Meet me at the Bitter End Bar tonight for a night you won't forget."*

"Talk about last minute planning," she said out loud.

She went to her bathroom, turned the bag of chips upside down, and the dope landed on top of them. She got out the syringe and lighter, but something inside her made her stop. She stared at the mess and then looked in the mirror, and said, "Renee, you don't need to do this." She then hurried downstairs, and out the kitchen door.

Thirty minutes later Jaylon arrived home. "Good, she's here," he said, seeing her car in the driveway.

"Renee!" he hollered, as he walked inside.

When there was no reply, he checked the living room thinking she might be asleep on the couch, but she wasn't there. He then went upstairs, and her bedroom door was open.

"Renee," he said, walking in.

She wasn't there, either. And as he turned to leave, he stopped dead in his tracks, horrified. A syringe, a lighter, and a small piece of folded foil, lay on the bathroom counter. Anger infused him. He unwrapped the foil and flushed the dope down the toilet. He then smashed the syringe on the floor with his foot and grabbed the lighter. When he turned to go downstairs, he noticed a piece of red ribbon hanging out of the top dresser drawer.

"Please don't tell me you spent the money on dope," he said, upset. He opened the drawer and took the envelope out, but he couldn't open it. He couldn't stand the thought of her doing that. He put the envelope back in the drawer and then left to go look for her.

After an hour of driving through the city streets, and with no luck finding her, he stopped at a convenience store. He grabbed a coke from the cooler in the back of the store, and when he went to pay for it, the cashier was talking to a friend about a party going down at the Bitter End Bar.

"That is going to be one wild party," the cashier said, looking at Jaylon.

Jaylon laid two bucks on the counter. "Why is that?"

"It's Ricky's party," the cashier quipped.

"Ricky? Who is Ricky?" Jaylon asked.

As he handed Jaylon his changed, he realized who he was talking to. "Hey! You're Jaylon MacKie. Dude, I love your music. Your band is what I call a true hard rock band."

Jaylon sort of smiled while trying not to laugh. "Thank you. Always nice to hear that."

"I'm surprised that Mr. Rock star doesn't know about Ricky," his friend said. "He's what you would call an elite dealer, high class, big bucks."

Jaylon looked him dead straight in the eyes, and said, "I don't know who this Ricky is, and by the sound of the party I don't want to know him. This rock star has always been clean and always will be. I have never tolerated drugs or that kind of lifestyle. Have a good evening." And he left.

He sat with the engine idling thinking about what the one guy had said. Right then, he remembered there was a guy named Ricky that hung out backstage at a few of the music festivals on the east coast. Even though he and his band never saw Ricky, they knew why he was there, and they didn't want anything to do with a drug dealer.

He shifted into drive, and muttered, "Ricky was the name of the guy at the dinner." He drove out of the store's parking lot and then laughed. "Dude? Real hard rock music? At least that dude likes my music."

Chapter Twelve

The Bitter End Bar was in full party mode. Ricky walked out of the room from where his party was being held and immediately saw Renee. He went over to her and handed his drink to her. "It's your favorite. Vodka."

She took a sip and chocked. "This is loaded."

"And that is just the beginning." He took her hand, but she hesitated, unsure if she really wanted to be here. "Don't worry, nobody is going to mess with you."

He led her through the crowded room, and as they neared his table, a girl who was sitting at another table suddenly stood up and bumped into Renee. "Watch it!" the girl snapped.

Ricky tugged on Renee's hand to keep her moving. He didn't want trouble.

The girl nudged her boyfriend and said. "That girl with Ricky, she doesn't belong here."

He shrugged his shoulders and said, "How would you know that?"

"I just do. Call it gut instinct. But she is in the wrong place."

"Let's do this right," Ricky said to Renee as they sat at his table.

"Here?" she said, thinking he was crazy. "People are around."

"You think anybody cares what we do? In a few minutes, you're not going to care, either. Besides, it's my party."

She was too busy looking around the room that she didn't hear what he had just said. A few seconds later, and with no warning, she felt a sharp jab in the bend of her left arm. "Take it easy!" she snapped.

"Watch out. You'll get a big rush. Just might smack you dead, too."

Not giving much thought to his comment, she stood up and grinned feeling electric energy shoot through her body.

Ricky laughed hard, and said, "Happy late New Year!" And then, quick as a heartbeat, he disappeared into the crowd.

Renee wove her way around the room as people danced under the strobe lights to the pulsating music. And for a moment she felt her body sway in sync to the rhythm of the flickering lights. She spread her arms out feeling ever so grandiose, and as though she was floating above everyone.

Suddenly, the feeling left. She stood in place, unable to focus on what was coming at her. A guy began groping up against her. She tried to shove him away, but he kept coming at her. Next thing she knew, Ricky threw him against the wall. The guy didn't get up. He didn't even try.

"I told you I wouldn't let anyone mess with you," Ricky said.

She stared at him blankly, and the room felt like it was spinning out of control. And then her body went limp.

"Whoa, my lady," he said, hanging onto her. He helped her walk back to their table and said, "What'd ya think?"

She didn't answer him. She put her hands on her head

trying to make the spinning stop, but the dope was in overdrive. Not knowing what to do, she stood up and leaned against the wall behind her, but her legs buckled under her.

Ricky watched her body slide down the wall and onto the floor. He crouched down in front of her knowing she needed help, but he wasn't about to stick around for her.

"Help me, God!" she screamed above the blaring music.

Ricky laughed and sneered, "There is no God, and nobody here is going to help you."

But he was wrong. The girl that bumped into her earlier heard her cry for help. She looked around wondering where the scream came from, but her boyfriend pulled her back to him.

"Stop pulling on me! It's the girl. I know it is."

"There's no way you could have heard her over the music," her boyfriend said, aggravated. "Let's get out of here."

In the meantime, Ricky was making his exit. And through the small slits of Renee's eyes, she watched him back away from her and then everything went black.

By then everyone had left. So, the girl went over to Renee and kneeled beside her. "Wake up!" she said, shaking her. "Wake up!"

Renee's eyes flashed open for a split second, and she caught a glimpse of the girl.

The girl's boyfriend grabbed her arm. "Just leave her alone. We need to get out of here!"

The girl was a Christian, a backsliding one at that, and now of all times, God was telling her to help Renee. "No! I have to help her. It's what God wants me to do."

Her boyfriend shook his head aggravated and then laughed, "You're stoned. Of course, you're going to hear God."

"You're the one who's stoned," she said, calling 911. "I haven't been using or drinking."

He tried to take her phone, but she held it away from him. "Go ahead. Make your call, but don't give them your name," he demanded.

After she explained to the dispatcher what had happened, the dispatcher asked for her name, but she had already hung up.

Her boyfriend grabbed her arm again, but she didn't budge.

"I want to make sure she is going to get help."

"No. You're crazy to hang around. The cops may show up."

"Go ahead and leave, but I'm staying."

"I'm not taking the chance of getting arrested," he said. And he exited out a side door.

Moments later, the owner of the bar came into the room, and the girl slipped out the same side door, but she kept it open just enough to see inside.

"Great. Just great! This is all I need. A girl passed out on the floor," the owner said.

He called 911 only to find out someone had already done so.

The girl smiled knowing she had done the right thing.

"Maybe I need to make a drastic change with my life," she muttered while walking to her boyfriend's car. "This life I'm living now isn't going anywhere but south, and that could've been me on the floor, as well."

Chapter Thirteen

Shane Kjierston walked through the lower wing of Bay Side Hospital carrying three large coffees in a cardboard drink tray. He stopped at the double doors, unclipped his I.D. badge from his shirt pocket, and swiped it through the security box. When the doors opened music was playing through the intercom, and all the rooms were empty which he found unusual. The ER was always nonstop hectic, but not at this morning hour of four o'clock.

Two nurses sat behind the nurse's station. One of them looked up at him and smiled.

"This is rare. Its calm down here," Shane said.

"Yes, it is. And it's rather nice for a change," the nurse said.

He passed by the rest of the staff and went to the second station where Dr. Kohl MacKie sat looking through a local music magazine. He preferred to be called Kohl, or Dr. Kohl, because of his last name. There have been many instances where patients figured out that he was Jaylon MacKie's brother which always made for awkward situations.

Kohl scratched the blonde stubble on his cheek and yawned, when he heard, "Here you go." Shane set the tray down. "It's dead down here." He stirred cream and sugar into his coffee with a red stir stick. Not getting a reply, he quipped, "Jaylon in that issue?"

"Yeah. And it is rather nice for a change," Kohl muttered. "And no, not in this issue."

"So," he said curiously.

Kohl took a sip of his coffee and looked at him. "So, what?"

"When are you going to give this up? The fifth floor is calling your name. You know Dr. Lunki wants you to be part of his team." Shane knew Kohl was tired of working in the ER, and he had mentioned a few times about working for Dr. Jo Lunki.

Kohl took the last cup from the tray and nodded towards the dispatcher's station. "This way."

"Here's your coffee, Steven."

"Thank you. It's too quiet down here. Maybe this coffee will help me stay awake." He took a few sips when a call came through of a possible overdose. "Coffee's working already."

"Breaks over everyone!" Kohl said. He set his cup down and hurried outside.

The ambulance's siren echoed through the hospital campus until it came to an abrupt stop beside him. The EMT stepped out of the back, and as he pulled the gurney out he said, "She's coding!"

Kohl climbed onto the gurney and begun CPR. "Let's go. Bay three."

"We are assuming she overdosed. Nobody was around to give us any info, or a name. So, we couldn't administer any meds. No Narcan, or the like," the EMT said.

Shane saw the lifeless body as they passed by him, and he

thought he recognized her from an appointment she had with Dr. Lunki several months ago.

"She's back," Kohl said. "I need blood work, and an IV of fluids started sooner than ASAP!"

Shane exhaled with relief, and he went back to the fifth floor.

Kohl looked over at the EMT and started to speak, but he couldn't. He had seen a lot of gruesome sights in the ER, but the girl that lay before him got to him in a way that no other patient had.

A nurse rushed in, and upon seeing the girls left arm, she said, "Where am I, or how am I..." and she stopped talking.

Kohl looked at her bruised and infected arm that Ricky had shot the lethal speedball into and said, "Somewhere between the blood crusted track is a vein. You'll just have to dig for one."

"The owner of a bar found her just as he was closing," the EMT said. He ruffled through a few papers. "The Bitter End Bar. That Place needs to be shut down. The cops won't even go to that area."

Renee lay on the gurney like a rag doll, and through her blurred vision, people were moving about like crazy bats while their voices echoed in the pit of her brain. And then, she coded, again.

"Not on my shift! Breathe!" Kohl said, applying CPR. And with one more lifesaving push, she inhaled hard and sat up. Everything spun in circles causing her to throw up several times over.

"No need for charcoal," the nurse said.

Renee laid back and then tried to sit up, but Kohl pushed her back down. She tried, again, but the nurse had tied her wrists to the gurney.

"What's your name?" Kohl asked her.

Her vision had cleared just enough for her to notice his blonde waves, but his amber eyes were what kept her attention. "Get off of me," she said angrily.

He got down and looked toward the hallway. "I need her lab results now. Someone needs to go find out what's taking so long."

A few seconds later, a nurse slipped around the curtain and handed Kohl a paper. It was all he could do to keep from showing emotion as he read over the lab results. Given the amount of heroin and coke that was in her body, he couldn't figure out how this girl was still alive.

He sighed hard. "You must have an angel watching over you. You've injected quite a bit cocaine and heroin and drank alcohol. You should be dead." He looked at the needle puncture on her arm. "Do you always mainline?"

"Looks that way," she muttered, hateful. She tried to move, but he held one leg down, while a nurse held the other leg. "Let go of me."

In the meantime, Shane was explaining to Dr. Lunki about the girl he saw in the ER. "She looked like death warmed over," Shane said to him. "But she reminded me of someone that came in to see you several months ago. Wait. She's the girl from New York."

Dr. Lunki looked at him hoping he misunderstood. "Are you sure that is who it was?"

"Yes."

"I'll be back."

He rushed down to the ER, found the room Renee was in, and said, "She is one of my patients."

"Good, then you can tell me her name," Kohl said.

"Renee Nolan," Dr. Lunki said.

"After tonight, I'm closer to making my decision about working for you." Kohl keyed in her name on the computer in the room and searched through her medical records. "She has no emergency contact info."

"That's right. She didn't want any contact info in her medical records, but she did give me a name and phone number to set aside for extreme emergencies."

Renee didn't give any contact numbers at her initial visit with Dr. Lunki. She even went as far to ask him to remove any contacts that were in her medical records.

Dr. Lunki wanted to ask her why she had let this happen, but he knew it wasn't the right time. So, instead, he asked, "Do you want me to call the number you gave me?"

"Yes," she said.

In the meantime, Jaylon had dozed off on the sofa while waiting for Renee to come home. When he woke up, his eyes focused on the gold lettering of a bible sitting on the shelf.

He took the Bible from the shelf, opened it to the book of Psalms, and read a few comforting verses. He repeated them several times over, and then he prayed for comfort and protection over Renee. And as he closed the Bible, his phone rang. "Renee," he answered, frantic.

"This is Dr. Lunki calling from Bay Side Hospital ER. Is this Jaylon MacKie?"

Jaylon's heart sank, afraid to hear what he about to tell him. "Yes, it is."

"Renee was brought to the ER this morning by ambulance. She overdosed, but she is alive."

"Thank God," Jaylon said, relieved. "I was afraid this was going to happen. I had a feeling that she was into something bad, but I had no proof until tonight. I found heroin and a syringe on her bathroom counter."

"That's how it goes a lot of times."

"I'm on my way there," Jaylon said.

"Renee gave me your number to set aside from her medical

and personal information. She respects your privacy, and so do I, but people around here may not. So, stay put for now. I will call you when I know more," Dr. Lunki said, as a call came through from Shane. "I have to go. I promise I will call you."

He hurried back to Renee's room and asked Kohl to come out into the hallway. "I'm calling Ryan from the rehab unit to talk to her. Sometimes he stays overnight, so let's hope he's here. Also, please know that I am not trying to interfere with your job. Just promise me you won't let her leave till Ryan talks with her, even if it's later today."

"You're not interfering," Kohl said.

Kohl went back and stayed right with her, afraid that her heart would stop beating, again. He has always shown concern for his patients, but there was more than just concern for her, he felt an attachment to her.

Renee dozed off only to wake up several hours later, and she saw someone else was sitting beside her.

"Hello. I'm Dr. Ryan Payne from the rehab unit. I was told you were left for dead at a bar. From what your blood work showed, your speedball was a time bomb waiting to go off. You're very fortunate it didn't because most generally it would have," he said.

"I want to leave, now!"

Kohl gave her a look that reminded her of Jaylon, and how he would look at her when he was frustrated with her.

"Listen. I run a short-term recovery home for addicts, and Dr. Lunki thinks it would be a good idea for you to go with me. If you don't get help now, next time you will be six feet under."

"I don't need your help. This wasn't supposed to have happened. I need to go home."

Ryan remained patient with her. He wasn't going to give up so quickly. He just couldn't believe that she was alive and that she was doing as well as she was. This was a miracle, indeed.

He and Kohl talked with her for nearly an hour, when she finally said, "Ok. I'll go, but I have to call home."

"Dr. Lunki called home for you," Kohl said, "and he will call, again, to let them know what's going on." He then sent Dr. Lunki a text letting him know that Renee was going to Ryan's rehab.

In the meantime, Jaylon was getting even more frustrated. He wanted to go to the hospital, but there was always a chance that someone would recognize him and ask for an autograph, or want their picture taken with him. And this wasn't the time for that.

He flipped through the TV channels for the umpteenth time when his phone rang, again. "Is she ok?" Jaylon answered.

"Yes," Dr. Lunki said. "Dr. Ryan Payne is one of the doctors in the addictions unit. He and his wife run a short-term private rehab in their home."

"I know him. We have been friends for a while," Jaylon said.

"He spoke with her, and she agreed to go there. Dr. Payne will call you as soon as she is settled."

"Thank you, doctor."

"You're welcome." And he hung up.

"Thank you, Jesus," Jaylon muttered. "I need to get in the habit of reading my bible, again."

Chapter Fourteen

A cold gust of wind and rain greeted Ryan and Renee as they arrived at Higher Ground Recovery. The moment she got out of the car, reality had hit home. She shivered as her eyes followed the brick sidewalk that leads to the wooden porch of the Victorian house. This would be the perfect time to run off and find Ricky, she thought. But she just stood there, sick from the absence of her bitter friend running through her veins.

Ryan kept his eyes on her the whole time. He knew from his own experience what was going through her head at this very moment. "It's normal to have second thoughts. Come on," he coaxed. "It's too cold to be standing out."

Drops of rain fell from the tree limbs, hitting her left cheek. She looked toward the sky, and between the gray clouds, a spot of sunlight was peeking through them.

"Do you see that?" she asked Ryan. He didn't see what she was looking at. "I'll do this for you guys," she muttered, looking into the sunlight.

He walked behind her as she started toward the house. But

right as she got to the edge of the porch, she made a mad dash up the street. Ryan ran after her for a few blocks, but it was no use, and he hurried back to the house.

"Renee just took off running up the street," he said to his wife, Brenda. "I tried to go after her, but she was too fast. I have no idea where that burst of energy came from, especially given the terrible condition she is in. We have to pray for her to return."

Immediately, they sat on the sofa, and hand in hand, Ryan began to pray. "Heavenly Father, we ask that you watch over Renee, protect her, and bring her back for treatment."

"Thank you, Jesus. Amen," Brenda prayed.

Renee may have taken off with a burst of energy, but she didn't get very far. She ended up at a small wooded park where she hid behind a tree and threw up several times over.

"What have I done!" she muttered to herself. "God, this wasn't supposed to have happened!" she said, yelling into the sky. "Ricky did this to me."

She made her way to a park bench and sat down. A hard shiver overtook her, as her hair and clothes were soaked from the cold rain and withdrawals.

"God, where are you?" she pleaded. And right then, a warm sensation touched the top of her head. She looked around and then into the sky where another spot of sunlight peaked through the clouds. She then realized that the rain was falling all around her, but not on her. She looked up, again, and the sunlight was brighter, spreading warmth throughout her body.

"This isn't just one of those things that happen," she muttered. "God, if this is your way of telling me that everything will get better, then give me the strength to walk back to the rehab house. Also, tell my kids I love them."

Fifteen minutes later, Renee stood at the edge of the brick

sidewalk reading the sign on the door. "Higher Ground Recovery. A Short-Term Rehab Home," she said to herself.

Brenda looked out the window. "She's back, Ryan."

Ryan opened the door, and she walked onto the porch. "I..." was all she could say as tears slid down her face.

"It's ok," he said, grinning. "You came back.

"God always answers prayers," Brenda said as she hugged her. "I'm so relieved you came back. It will get better over the next few weeks.

Renee smiled, and said, "I know it will because God gave me the strength to walk back.

Chapter Fifteen
Four Weeks Later

Shane had left Jaylon's house a half hour ago. He had brought a burger and fries for himself, and a coke for the two of them. He also filled Jaylon in about the morning Renee was in the ER.

Jaylon downed the last of his coke and then stretched out on the sofa hearing Shane's last words, 'Face it. You love her', repeat through his mind. He then drifted off to sleep only to be woken up from a loud knock at the front door. He ambled over to the door and opened it.

"Hi. Come in. What brings you here?" he asked his parents, yawning.

"We decided to go for a drive, so we thought we would stop by," Dave said, looking at the take-out sacks on the coffee table. "Joleys?"

"Shane came over and brought his supper, and a coke for me, before going to work. I wasn't in the mood to eat."

"We haven't seen or heard from you in a few weeks. That's

not like you," Natalie said.

"Funny you stopped by," he said. "I was going to call you later. Several weeks ago, I asked you to pray for Renee because I was worried that she might be into something bad." He cleared his throat and scratched the back of his head, unsure how to say what he needed to say. "She is in a private rehab. Ryan's, as a matter of fact. She has been using narcotic pain meds since before she moved up here, and several months ago she started using heroin. Anyway, she almost died of an overdose."

Natalie gasped. "Oh no! Is she ok?"

"Yes. Her doctor told me she was at a bar, and she or someone filled her vein with a lethal speedball."

Natalie frowned, not knowing what a speedball was.

"That's heroin and coke together," Jaylon said.

"Thank God she is ok."

"Pastor Benny, Natalie, and I have been praying for her," Dave said.

"She's been there for few weeks. I would have told you sooner, but she is so private that I have kept quiet about it. But at the same time, I figured you should know since you care about her so much."

"God has placed her in good hands. Ryan and Brenda will take care of her," Dave said. "Now, on another note, I'm hungry. Why don't the three of us go get some supper, and we can discuss this more?"

"I haven't heard from her yet, so I'm hoping she will call any day now," he said as he walked down the hallway to get his jacket. When he came back to the living room, his house phone rang.

Before he could even finish saying hello, Renee said, "Hi! I couldn't wait to call someone, so tag you're it. Besides, I don't know who else to call, well besides..." and she stopped talking as Ricky's name almost escaped her lips.

"Mom and dad came over, and we were just leaving to go eat. I hope you don't mind, but I told them about you."

"It's ok. I'm getting along great. The first week was really rough, but I got through it. I'm just glad I got help now, or it would have been a lot harder for me. Ryan said he would release me to go home in the next few weeks."

"Good," Jaylon said. "I look forward to that day."

"Me, too. I'll let you go now. Eat something good for me. Talk to you later."

After they hung, he looked at his mom and dad and grinned. "Joleys?"

Chapter Sixteen

Three Weeks Later

It was six p.m. on a Saturday evening. Renee paced the living room floor of the rehab waiting on Jaylon to pick her up. Every few minutes she would look out the window thinking she had heard someone walk onto the porch. Frustrated, she sat down only to hear a knock on the door.

The moment she opened the door, Jaylon hugged her. "It's about time you get to come home."

Ryan and Brenda came down the hallway. "Hi, Jaylon. I think Renee and I have taken care of any last-minute details," Ryan said.

"I think so, too," Renee said.

"Wait. I almost forgot something," Ryan said. He went to his office and returned with a small book. "This book is filled with bible verses. I used a yellow highlighter on certain ones that really helped me, and I know they will help you, as well. And, I know I have told you this several times, but you are very fortunate to have gotten help as soon as you did. Your addiction would have grown deeper, and your treatment would have been long-term, and much harder to recover from unless it succumbed you first."

"I know. Thank you, both," she said to Ryan and Brenda.

The moment Renee and Jaylon walked out the door a huge grin came over her face.

Seeing the look of awe on her face, he shrugged his shoulders, and said, "One of the perks of being a rock star."

"A dark red Jaguar. When did you get it?"

"I guess that means you never looked in the garage," he said, opening the passengers' door for her.

"Never had a reason to."

"I hope you're hungry."

"Very."

He drove out of town, heading north-west. She knew where he was taking her.

"What if I had said I wasn't hungry?"

He chuckled. "You would never turn down Italian food."

Twenty minutes later they arrived at The Authentic Italian Restaurant. The same waiter they had the last time they were there lead them to a private room in the back.

"Surprise!" his family said as they entered the room.

"We all wanted to celebrate you, and your sobriety," Jaylon said.

"How nice. Thank you!" Renee said as she sat down.

Dave led them in a prayer and then said a toast. "We are so happy, and thankful, that you are here with us. We have been praying for God to watch over you, and to give you comfort and healing. So, this night is for you and to let you know we love you very much."

For the rest of the evening, they laughed and joked with each other, and talked about everything except her time at Ryan's, which made the night that much better. Opening to

Ryan about certain things was hard enough, let alone going through the first week of detox.

When they had finished eating, Natalie and Dave gave her their cell phone numbers and told her to call anytime, no matter what hour it was.

Dyllon came over and hugged her, and then he told his grandma and grandpa that he was going with Jaylon and Renee to their house.

When they arrived home, she went straight to her bedroom. The bathroom door was open, and the counter had been cleaned off. This is where that horrible night all began, she thought. How stupid of me. "None of this would have happened if I hadn't...I would be dead, or near dead if that night had not happened," she mumbled as she stretched out on the bed. And then she vaguely remembered a girl who was trying to help her. "Where did she come from?" And she drifted off to sleep.

In the meantime, Dyllon grabbed the TV remote and begun flipping through the channels. "You think she is going to be ok?" he asked his dad.

"Yes, I do."

"I thought she would have been in rehab longer."

"Ryan's is a short-term rehab house. She had been using narcotic pain meds since before she moved up here, and the heroin didn't come into play until the last several months. So, it's not like someone who has been a hard-core user for years. Either way, it's going to take her a while to completely heal. But with us as support, and Ryan and Brenda, I think she will be fine."

"I'm surprised she was able to do her job," Dyllon said.

"From what I understand, she would finish cleaning for the day and then use. So, I guess that gave her the following day off to sober up. I was usually gone, so I didn't know what was going on."

"Guess that's what they call a functional addict," Dyllon said. "You love her?"

Jaylon looked at him for a few seconds and then realized what he had just asked. "Do I love her?" he asked, shocked. "Renee and I have already discussed this. I'm not ready for a relationship."

"Reighanna seems to think so."

"Well, you know your sister. She can make something out of nothing."

Dyllon gave a quick laugh. "Yeah, and especially if it's none of her business. She always waits for the right time, which is usually the wrong time, or when it doesn't matter anymore.

"Yup. She misses her mom. I guess that's her way of dealing with it. I'm going upstairs to see if Renee is ok."

"Someone will snatch her away from you if you wait too long," Dyllon teased as Jaylon left the room.

Jaylon tapped lightly on her bedroom door, walked in, and saw that she was sound asleep. He touched her cheek with the back of his hand to make sure she was breathing. Her skin was warm to the touch. He then took the blanket from the end of the bed and covered her with it, and he went back downstairs.

Several hours later she woke up soaked in sweat and craving her bitter friend. "Four a.m.," she muttered, squinting at the time on her phone. She then took a quick shower, dressed in fresh clothes, and went downstairs.

She flipped through the TV channels as emotions and feelings that she hadn't felt for a long time surround her. She knew what would take all this away, heroin. And then she remembered Dave and Natalie telling her to call anytime.

Dave's number was the first on the small piece of paper that Natalie had given her at the restaurant. "It's almost five in the morning, and you are calling Jaylon's dad," she muttered to herself. After two rings she changed her mind, and she hung up.

"Hello," Dave answered, hearing a click on the other end. He looked at the caller I.D. and hit redial.

"Hello," she answered.

"Renee are you ok?" Dave asked concerned.

"I'm sorry. I shouldn't have called, especially at this hour."

"Natalie and I consider you family, and we told you to call any time. Besides, I couldn't sleep knowing that I had to be at work early, so I was fixing a pot of coffee."

"I woke up and couldn't go back to sleep. Yeah, I... these feelings and emotions are filling my head, and I can't seem to make them stop."

"You are bound to feel uneasy. From what I know about addiction, it takes time to retrain, if that is the word I want to use, your thought process. I am guessing here because Jaylon hasn't told us much about what happened. You don't have to go through this alone, nor do you need to beat yourself up over this. We all mess up, intentionally or not. In God's eyes, no sin is greater, or no less, than another. It's all the same, and he forgives. I am not sure if you believe in God, but you should reach out to Him."

"I accepted Christ as my savior when I was a child. It wasn't until I was an adult that I developed a more personal relationship with Him. After things happened in New York, I felt alone, and that God wasn't with me, anymore." She hesitated, trying to hold back frustration. "This isn't coming out right. I love God, and I need to reestablish my relationship with Him. But for now, all I can do is write to Him in my journal, and maybe someday I will pick up my bible again." Right then, her nerves calmed down, and the craving ceased. "I think I am going to go back to sleep, now. Thank you for listening."

"We are here for you. Get some rest," Dave said and hung he up.

An hour later, Jaylon's alarm clock beeped for several seconds. He rolled over and slammed it off with the palm of his hand.

As he made his way down the hallway, he saw that Renee's bedroom door was open. He peered around the doorway, and he panicked, seeing she wasn't there. He then hurried down to the living room where she was sleeping on the sofa. "Ok, calm down, she's ok," he said.

Minutes later, Renee aroused to the smell of bacon and eggs.

"Sit down. I fixed breakfast for all of us," Jaylon said as she came into the kitchen.

She filled her mug with coffee while Jaylon scooted eggs from the frying pan onto their plates. He then set a plate of bacon in the center of the table.

"I should be the one fixing you breakfast," she said.

"When I woke up, I saw your bedroom door was open. I panicked, thinking you might have left during the night to go meet someone."

She knew he meant Ricky. "Four a.m. rolled around, and I couldn't go back to sleep. So, I came downstairs and watched TV. But believe me, the thought was there."

"I need to ask you something," Jaylon said. "Is there any more dope in the house, anywhere?"

"No. I'm sorry for bringing it into your home. I had every intention of using it that night, but something stopped me."

"Consider that an act of God watching over you, and in more ways than one. If you had used it, and as much as you or whoever shot into your vein, you probably wouldn't be alive. I hope you erased your dealer's number from your phone."

"The way it all came down, I had no idea the person was

going to use that much. I wasn't looking."

"You weren't looking?" Jaylon said, aggravated.

"The person grabbed my arm when I wasn't looking, and before I could do anything about it, it was too late. And I don't need my dealer's number on my phone. It's etched in my brain."

"Anyway. Moving on. Since this is your first day back, I'd like to stay with you, but I have meetings to go to, and I have to drop Dyllon off at school."

"I heard my name," Dyllon said as he came into the kitchen.

"Jaylon I am thirty-ei...I will be ok. Your number is etched in my brain, as well."

Jaylon gave her a quick hug. "It's all over now," he said, and he went upstairs.

Dyllon scarfed down his breakfast and just in time for Jaylon to come back down. "Come on Dyllon. We gotta go."

Dyllon set his dishes in the sink and then hugged Renee. "Have a good day."

"Thank you. You, too," Renee said as Dyllon and Jaylon walked out the door.

Chapter Seventeen

West Bay Library was not far from Jaylon's house. It seemed to be the only place where Renee could hibernate without interruption. As long as she kept her hands busy, whether it was turning the pages of a book or writing in her journal, the thoughts of using were not as bad. But instead of finding a nook to sit in, she checked her books out and headed back to the house.

She took four Ibuprofen and settled down on the sofa. For several weeks now, she had been feeling pain in her joints and muscles. She had put off calling Dr. Lunki because she wanted to try and deal with it on her own. Heroin and the narcotic pain relievers had numbed her pain so much that now the OTC meds do not help her.

"I might as well call his office. Maybe I can get in today," she muttered, tossing her book aside.

After she made the appointment, she grabbed her book and stretched out on the sofa. It wasn't long before her eyes grew heavy, and she dozed off only to wake up an hour later to the sound of ruffling paper.

Jaylon was sitting in the recliner reading the local newspaper. "Your book is on the table. There is a mug of coffee for you, and a cinnamon roll, as well. The coffee is a new Italian blend from Laurens Bakery. I thought you would like it."

She took a bite of the roll, and then a few sips of coffee. "This is really good. By the way, I have an appointment with my doctor today. This pain won't let up. His receptionist did her magic and worked me in."

"Probably a good idea," he said, keeping his eyes on the paper. "Do you need me to go with you?"

"No. I appreciate the offer, though."

He smiled and kept reading.

"Are you looking for another housekeeper?"

He darted a blank look at her. "No. Why would you think that?"

She smiled, picked up her mug and roll, and left the room.

By three that afternoon, she was on the elevator that went straight to Dr. Lunki's floor. And today, she was more than thankful for the elevator as her pain begun to wreak havoc.

Seconds later, the doors opened, and her body tensed up. Charlene, his receptionist, was at the nurse's station and noticed that Rene was in trouble, and she rushed over with a wheelchair.

Dr. Lunki came around the corner of the desk. "Bring her around," he said and led them to a room down the hall.

"I guess this is payback for shooting junk into my veins," Renee said. "I'm not sure if the pain feels worse because I've been numb to it for so long, or if it really is worse. If there were such a thing as a good time to relapse, it would be now." He knew what she meant but didn't reply. "This makes me nervous," she said as a nurse came into the room to draw her blood.

"Renee, I know your blood work will be clean," he said, "but I'm checking for other things, as well. Because you're an addict, I can't just give you anything. Which means I won't send you home with just any kind of pain medicine. Oh, by the way, I heard you made it through rehab without the use of Suboxone and the like. I'm just glad you got help as soon as you did."

"Me, too," she said.

A half-hour later, an IV was inserted into her arm and tapped down. A small amount of blood seeped through the tape reminding her of the moments before shooting up. That's when bittersweet relief was on the way. Only this time it was a low dose of Morphine.

"Remember me? From the ER?" Kohl said, walking into her room.

Renee looked up and realized who he was. How could I not remember you? she thought. Blonde beard, and lose blonde curls, but it was his amber eyes that caught her attention. There was something about them that stood out, but she just couldn't figure out what it was. Kohl didn't look enough like Jaylon for her to think that they may be related.

"Renee, right?" He sat in the recliner next to her and made sure the medicine was dripping down into the IV. "By the way, I'm Kohl. Hope you don't mind that I'm here."

"No. No. That's ok," she said, trying not to sound giddy. "So, what brings you here?"

Kohl explained that he had quit the ER and that he now works for Dr. Lunki, or as everyone on the fifth floor calls him, Dr. Jo.

"So, the last time I saw you, you were walking out of the ER with Dr. Ryan Payne. I had asked Dr. Jo a few times how you were doing, but you sitting here tells me you are recovering well."

"I'm doing better than I thought I would have. Ryan and Brenda, and the guy I live with, along with his family, have been a huge help."

"You live with your boyfriend?" he asked, trying not to sound disappointed.

"No. He is not my boyfriend. It's kind of a long story."

"We have nothing to do for a few hours. Or, I mean, I'm not busy, and you're not going anywhere for a while."

She smiled, and said, "Ok. I live with my boss. I'm his housekeeper. He left town for a few months, and he asked me to stay at his place while he was gone. He didn't want to worry about me being alone." She laughed under her breath, and said, "In other words, he has more reliable neighbors."

Kohl sort of chuckled. "Sounds like someone I know."

"He was in the process of buying a house, and he asked me to go there, as well. So, he thought I might as well go ahead and move in with him. But there is no relationship or anything like that between us."

"That's good," he said. His face tinged a shade of pink. "Or, I mean, it's good he is like that with you."

"Hi," Dr. Jo said walking into the room. "You are going to come back four times a week, for two weeks, to help you get through this bad phase."

"Considering Morphine and heroin are opiates, I would have thought I'd feel some sort of rush. But I didn't get that, or even a sense of peace. In fact, I don't like it."

"That's a good thing," he said. "You may have a brief period where the medicine wears off before you come back. Call me ASAP if you have any side effects, and I will be calling between visits to make sure you're doing ok, as well. When you are done with the treatments, I will have something for you to take at home when needed."

She didn't mind coming back, especially if it meant getting to see Kohl.

When her treatment was finished, Kohl walked her to the elevator. "See you in a few days.

She turned and grinned. "I can't wait."

He smiled and wanted to kiss her, but instead, he reached inside the door and pressed the first-floor button.

"I can't wait," she garbled, as the elevator lowered. "Why did you say that? How stupid."

Kohl sat behind the nurse's desk flipping through a magazine. He looked up only to see Charlene and Dr. Jo staring at him.

"What?" he said, with a slight chuckle.

Dr. Jo cleared his throat and said, "It's ok if you like her,"

"Honey, it shows," Charlene teased. "I would say you're in l-o-v-e."

Right then a patient's monitor beeped. "My saving grace," Kohl said, and he rushed down the hallway.

Renee went back every four days for the next two weeks. And Kohl stayed with her every time, and not just by coincidence, either.

When the last day of her appointments arrived, Kohl walked around the corner from his office and went to the nurses' station. "Did you call Renee to tell her that her appointment had been moved up an hour?" he asked Charlene.

"Yes, I did," she said, grinning.

Moments later, the elevator doors opened, and Renee saw Kohl. She thought this would be the last time she would get to see him, so she tried not to let the fact that she was upset show.

He went over to her, and without giving her a chance to speak, he took her hand, and said, "Come with me." He then led her to another elevator. "I'm hungry. I haven't eaten all day. Hope you don't mind joining me."

"Is this a date?" she joked.

He kissed her, and said, "We can call it that." When the doors opened, he tugged her hand to lead her to the cafeteria, but she just stood there mesmerized. He kissed her, again. "Come on."

"Pick anything you want, and as much as you want. I don't care," he said, grabbing two trays.

He loaded his tray with a turkey sandwich, two bags of chips, and a chocolate cupcake when he noticed the small bowl of salad and a roll on her tray. He then got two cokes from the cooler, paid the cashier, and led her to a table in the back of the cafeteria.

"Please don't tell me you are afraid to eat too much. I mean, I just find it funny that..." He sighed. "Never mind. I'm sorry."

"Nothing to be sorry about. I knew what you meant," she said as he cut his sandwich in half.

"I'm glad this spot was empty. I don't like being around people while I am eating. There's always a nosy person or someone who knows me that comes by while I'm trying to eat in peace."

"There is this bakery I want to stop by on the way home," she chimed in. "A few weeks ago, my boss bought this awesome coffee there from there. I like my coffee black. No lattes, cappuccinos, and no cream or sugar, just plain black coffee. They also have these amazing cinnamon rolls with lots of fluffy icing..." and she stopped talking, realizing she was babbling about something that had nothing to do with what he was talking about. And yet, he had the biggest grin on his face, listening to every word she said. "I'm sorry. I didn't mean to go on like that."

"It's ok. I like hearing you talk. Speaking of cinnamon rolls, I hope you have room to share my dessert with me."

He held the cupcake between two of his fingers. She

wrapped her fingers around his and took a bite. The corners of his lips moved upwards, and then he polished off the rest of it.

"I have redecorated my condo, and I would like an opinion on it. Maybe after your treatment, you could come over." He noticed the blank expression on her face. "What's wrong?"

"How's that going to work? I mean, you're working."

"Nope. It's my day off. I came here just to see you."

She grinned, feeling her heart melt. "Ok, then. I'll go. But I better go back up before Dr. Jo starts wondering where I'm at."

Back in the room, she sat in the recliner and propped her feet up. "I got caught up," she said as Dr. Jo came into the room.

He looked at Kohl and then at her, and grinned. "No problem at all."

Chapter Eighteen

"My car is over there," Kohl said, pointing to his right. It was more like way in the back over there. The closer they got to his car, the more she understood why he parked in the back of the parking garage. He opened the passenger's door for her, and she slipped into the seat of his black BMW Z4. He walked around the car, got behind the wheel, and drove to his condo.

She loved the warm, rich décor of his condo. A leather sofa, two recliners, and a sixty-inch flat screen TV set in the center of the room. And over by the dining area was a black baby grand piano.

"I just had the walls painted, and the carpet is new. A few people are coming to look at it next week."

"You're moving?" she asked. "And here we just met," she muttered under the breath.

He looked at her not understanding what she said. "What?"

"Nothing," she said disappointedly.

He couldn't understand the sudden change in her attitude.

And then the word moving hit him. He liked the idea that she didn't want him to move, but he knew he had better fix the situation before she got the notion to leave.

"I'm sorry. I should have explained sooner. I just bought a house in the country. No need to worry," he said and gave her a quick kiss. "I'll be right back." And he went upstairs.

Several minutes later, he came back wearing a pair of worn skinny jeans and a blue button-down shirt, leaving a few of the top buttons unbuttoned. He sat down beside her and turned on the TV. "So? What do you think?"

"Nice," she said. "Really nice. I mean, I love it." She swallowed hard. "Your condo, that is. Sweet piano, too."

"That's my baby. You'll get to hear her play plenty of times. You know, I'm hungry, again. And no more than you ate, you have to be hungry, as well. I have some left-over deli chicken. I'll be right back."

"Oh, shoot," she mumbled, realizing that she had not called Jaylon to let him know she might not be back for a while and not to worry. She sent him a text message and turned her phone to silent.

She tried to watch TV, but her mind was on Kohl. Everything about him turned her on. His smile, his smooth voice, his kindness, and especially what he was wearing on those long skinny legs. And right then, she went and joined him in the kitchen.

She snuck up behind him and snuggled against him. He sighed, as he liked the feeling of her warm embrace. But instead of giving into his desire for her, he turned around and kissed her. "I want things to be just right before making love to you." Not only did he want things right, but he also wanted them right before God.

They sat on the sofa watching repeats of Blue Bloods while talking into the night until she nodded off. He took the pillow he was leaning against and set it in his lap. "Here," he said. She laid her head on the pillow and stretched her legs out on the sofa.

He gently touched her face and ran his fingers down the side of her cheek. Her warm skin and silky dark hair sent a rush of sweet ecstasy through him. He hadn't felt this way in a long time, nor had he been on a date in a long time, and those dates bombed out. The girls were either fascinated with the fact that he was the brother of Jaylon MacKie the rock star, or they just wanted to party and make out.

He had rededicated his life to Christ three years ago, and he wasn't about to share himself with just anyone. He wanted a lady. A lady that was real, with feelings, and emotions, but most of all, to love him. He knew that lady was Renee from the moment they met a few weeks ago. In fact, he was in love with her the first time he saw her in the ER.

By the time the last episode of Blue Bloods ended, Renee was sound asleep. He gently raised her head, got up, and covered her with a blanket. He then stretched out in one of the recliners and fell asleep.

The following morning, he drove her back to the hospital parking lot.

When she got behind the wheel of her car, he leaned in and kissed her. "I'd like to see you again."

Did her heart ever skip a few beats. "I would like that, too."

"I'll call you tomorrow, and if my break permits, I'll call tonight."

"Ok. Let me find something to write my phone number on."

"I have it."

"You do? How?" The only people she had given her phone number to where Jaylon and Dr. Jo.

"One of the perks of my job. I got it from Dr. Jo's desk. We were going over patient files and entering information into the computer. When he opened your file, your number was laying on top of it. So, I entered it on my phone. But keep that between us."

"Oh. I see. Not a problem. I'll talk to you later tonight, or tomorrow."

He kissed her one last time, and she left.

When she arrived home, Jaylon noticed how happy she was. "You're glowing."

"W-well."

He laughed. "You're in deep. Are you going to tell me who the lucky man is?"

"Nope," she said as she went up to her room.

Later that night her phone rang, startling her awake, and she answered with a groggy, "Hello."

"Hi," Kohl said. "I happened to get a small break, and I couldn't wait to call."

"Glad you did. What time is it?"

"Eleven."

"Are you busy tonight?"

"Yeah. I have a feeling that the next few weeks are going to be that way, as well. A few people are on vacation which leaves the floor shorthanded. Dr. Jo relies on Shane and me to take up the slack."

"Shane?"

"He's an assistant to Dr. Jo. Anyway, I will make it up to you after this busy spell is over. Hang on a second," he said. She overheard him talking to Charlene about a patient. "Renee, I'm sorry, but I have to go now. I will try to call later, but it might be tomorrow. Bye-bye."

It was then that she remembered Kohl saying the word perks. "Perks?" she muttered. "Surely not. He can't be. He doesn't even look like Jaylon." She then set her phone on the nightstand and went back to sleep.

Three weeks had passed since she last saw Kohl. And to get her mind on something else, other than wondering when they were going to see each other, a long walk was her answer.

A brisk late winter breeze blew through her hair as she strolled along West Bay Avenue. She stopped to gaze at fine china in storefront window when her phone rang. "Hello," she answered, excited.

"I'd like to see you today," Kohl said. "Tell me where you live, and I'll pick you up."

"Great! Why don't I meet you at your place in a few hours?"

"Oh. Ok. I don't mind picking you up."

"It's just that I'm out walking, and it will take a bit to get home. I will call you when I am on my way to your place."

"Sure. No problem. I might run out in a few minutes to pick up some things at the store. See you when you get here."

"Yes! Finally," she said after he hung up. She then picked her pace up to a near run.

Thirty minutes later she arrived home, took a shower, and dressed in black jeans and a red shirt. And as she was leaving, she heard. "Where are you going?"

"To Ko... To see that guy that you're not going to meet anytime soon." And she hurried out the door before he could say another word.

Kohl didn't give Renee a chance to knock on the door. "About time!" he said, hugging her tight. "I missed you." He kissed her and shut the door behind them. "I have something for you." He walked over to the sofa where two dozen roses lay, and he handed them to her.

"These are gorgeous! Thank you! Wow!"

"Hope you're hungry. I got us a pizza."

On the dining room table were two place settings and two

candles. "Very nice," she said as he sat down at the piano.

"Have a seat," he said, patting the piano bench with his hand.

She sat next to him as he played a romantic tune. "I like it."

"Just something I came up with." He kissed her, again, and said, "Let's eat."

She laughed. "You're always hungry."

Later that evening they went for a long drive and ended up at the park. They sat on her favorite bench by the bay admiring the sunset.

"This is a great spot," he said, putting his arm around her. He leaned in to kiss her, but no sooner than his lips pressed against hers, she gasped and jumped up.

"What's wrong."

"I thought I saw someone's shadow flash behind us," she said, terrified.

"Who do you think it was?" Kohl said as he scanned the area.

"I don't know. Let's go back to your place."

"Sure," he said, concerned.

She had her suspicions that it was Ricky, but she wasn't going to talk about it.

When they returned to his condo, he said, "I don't mean to cut this evening short, but I have to be at work by seven in the morning." He did have to be at work by seven, but the incident in the park bothered him, as well. He had his suspicions that there was more to it than just mere coincidence.

"Ok. I have a feeling I need to get back home, anyway."

"Wait, don't forget these," he said, handing her the roses.

"Thank you for the roses. I love them."

Her smile sent a sweet chill through him, and he gave her a long passionate kiss. "I'll call you tomorrow."

When Renee returned home, she set the roses on the

kitchen table and went to the dining room, where Jaylon and a few friends were having drinks while he sipped on a coke.

She peeked around the corner at him and Stokie. And from what she could see Joleys sacks were on the table. "Hi," she said to Jaylon.

Jaylon got up and followed her to the kitchen. "Wow. Those are expensive gorgeous," he said, eyeing them. "Oh, by the way, we will be moving in a month. I hope, anyway."

"Ok. I'll get some boxes tomorrow. I'm going on up to bed." And as she turned to go upstairs, she noticed a slight jealous look on his face as he eyed the roses. "No. I'm not telling you who he is."

He gave a quiet laugh and went back to the dining room.

Chapter Nineteen

Six Weeks Later

It was a Thursday evening, and Renee was preparing to go see Kohl. She dressed in black jeans, a slinky purple blouse, and stilettos, and then she went down stairs.

Just as she started out the kitchen door, Jaylon walked in. "You're all dolled up. Must have a date."

"Yes. He usually works on Thursdays, so this was a surprise." She noticed the concerned look on his face. "Something wrong?"

"Yeah." He ran his hand through his hair and leaned against the kitchen counter. "What's the deal of you not wanting to tell me who he is? And he never comes over here or picks you up."

"Let me put it this way, in the past, I have been let down and lied to, and sometimes I blame myself because I didn't see it coming. Seeing him feels so real, so right, and I'm afraid if I say too much about him I will jinx it all. Heck, I don't even know his last name."

"Seriously? You don't know his last name? And how long have you been seeing him? What if he is friends with the wrong people?" He saw the hard frown on her face. "I'm sorry. I shouldn't have said that."

"I tell you what, if we get serious I will have him come here so you can meet him, but if we call it quits I will tell you who he is."

"Deal. Have a good time," he said as she walked out the door.

Kohl took Renee to a small café for a late evening meal. She talked about a few different things, but he said very little to her.

"You're quiet tonight. Everything ok?" she asked as he stirred cream and sugar into his coffee.

He set the spoon down, cleared his throat, and said, "I've been wondering about something.

"What?" she said, grinning.

"We have been seeing each other for two or three months now. I love being with you, but there is one thing that really bothers me."

"Ok," she said, seeing the concerned look in his eyes.

"Why won't you let me pick you at your house? I know you say it's nothing bad, but I can't help thinking that you are married to him? I know you say you're not, but still."

Her eyes widened, and her smile faded. "No. I am sorry all that bothers you. I understand why you question, though. But honestly, it is just that..." and she stopped talking, trying to figure out what to say. "Look. I plan on introducing you to him soon, just not now. That's all I can say. You will understand when you meet him. But wait a sec—"

"And the deal at the park a while back," he interrupted, "you practically jumped out of your skin. You wouldn't tell me who it was or explain it. Sort of makes me want to stand back, like something bad is waiting around the corner."

It was all she could do to stay calm. "I have wondered about your family. You have never talked about them. Heck, you haven't told me your last name, and yet I don't pressure you about it. I figured you would when you were ready."

"I know. I have been wanting to introduce you to my family, but with the way my schedule is, it's impossible." He looked out the window and thought for a moment. "Ok. You have a point, but I am not purposely hiding them."

"Oh really. I'm hiding him from you?"

"You're hiding something. I can feel it, and it bothers me. If you can't share it with me, then maybe we should . . ." and he stopped talking.

Renee picked at her food no longer in the mood to eat. Kohl finished eating, picked up the tab, and they left.

There was no long drive through the city or park. Just an unnerving quiet ride back to this condo.

He pulled up behind her car and looked over at her. "I have plans over the next few days that I can't change. I'll try to call you tomorrow."

Her heart sank, thinking all of this was her fault. She didn't know what to say. "Look. I am..." There was a look of don't say any more in his eyes. She got out of the car, and said, "You're being ridiculous which pretty well tells me I don't need you." And she slammed the door shut.

As she drove home, she was so upset that she didn't see the stop sign up ahead, when all the sudden, a car's horn blared as it passed in front of her. She gasped, and slammed the brakes on, coming to an abrupt stop. She then looked both ways twice, crossed the intersection, and pulled up along the curb to calm down.

"What the heck just happened with him? None of this makes any sense," she said, upset. And then she laughed. "This was all so stupid." But her laugh faded. "I guess he is not who I thought he was. This has all been a lie. Not real at all. Seems to be the story of my life."

When she arrived home, she hurried upstairs and slammed her bedroom door shut, as she was more irked at him than before. But the one thing she couldn't explain to him was the deal in the park. At first, she thought it was Ricky, but he had no reason to haunt her that way. And then the conversation she had with Detective Leary came to mind. She got his card out of her wallet, punched his number in on her phone.

After two rings he answered. "Hello."

"Is this Detective Leary?"

"Yes, it is."

"Oh good. This is Renee Nolan. I know it's nine at night, but you told me to call anytime."

"You're fine. Is everything ok?"

"Yes. Well, no. I had not heard from you in a while. I was wondering if you have any leads on finding the person," and she hesitated. For some reason, she was unable to say who killed my family.

"Every time we think we have a lead it turns out to be nothing, or our leads go into hiding knowing they are being pursued. Has something happened?"

Renee explained the incident at the park, and that she didn't think it was just kids playing tricks.

"Keep your eyes open, and be careful where you go alone," Detective Leary said. "I assure you that I am still working on this. And, again, if you have any ideas, or if anything else happens, do not hesitate to call, even if it's the wee hours of the morning."

"Ok. Thank you so much."

She wasn't about to tell him about Ricky. That could open up something mean and nasty. Ricky was not someone to mess with, and she was more than sure he had friends in dark places that would do his dirty work.

Later that night, Kohl woke up from a deep sleep. He turned the TV on, grabbed his phone, and debated on whether to call Renee. He knew he didn't handle the situation right, and that he was too quick in making accusations. He should have told her about his family, but he was afraid she would only like him because he was Jaylon's brother. Then again, he knew better, because she was different than other girls he had dated. He knew that she genuinely liked him, and maybe even loved him.

He punched in her number on his phone, but he hung up before it had a chance to ring.

"Maybe I should let it rest till tomorrow," he mumbled, and he set the phone on the nightstand and went back to sleep.

Chapter Twenty

Moving Day

Jaylon took down the glass frame in the upstairs hallway, bubble-wrapped it at least four times, and then put it in the back of the Escalade. He wasn't about to let anyone touch the frame or its precious contents, not even his friends who are going to help move the furniture in a few days.

In the meantime, Renee was in her room packing. She looked around the room, and then glimpsed at the bathroom vanity. In the back of one of the drawers was a small bundle of the sort, taped up beyond ridiculous. She racked her brain, trying to figure out when she would have done something like this, let alone what she might have put inside the bundled mess. The thought that it might be heroin went through her mind, but she never brought anymore into the house since the night of Ricky's party. She then heard the kitchen door shut, so she threw it into a box of random items, sealed it, and went downstairs.

As Jaylon and Renee packed books, CD's, and movies into

boxes, her silence was getting the best of him. She had not said but a few words to him the whole morning.

"My brother and I were beginning to think we would never get to buy the house. The previous owners had some legal issues that needed to be resolved before they could close on it. We sure waited long enough, though." He then realized she wasn't listening to a word he was saying. "I was in my room reading when I heard your bedroom door shut, or rather slam shut. Everything ok?"

Renee rested her hands on her waist. "Huh? Oh. Yeah," she sighed. "They guy I'm seeing just bought a house."

Jaylon gave her an odd look. "Hum. Your two favorite men bought a house at the same time." She didn't catch the joke, so he said, "Must be moving season, I guess. You sure you don't want to tell me who this guy is?"

She gave a shy smile and continued packing when her phone vibrated, but she ignored it. Several minutes later it vibrated, again.

"Hello," she answered impatiently.

"Hi. It's me," Kohl said. "You sound like you might be busy, so I'll make this quick. I'm sorry about last night. I didn't handle any of it right. In fact, I was rather stupid for making such a big deal out of everything."

She walked out onto the front porch and closed the door behind her. "I'm sorry, too."

"Anyway," he said, fumbling for words. "I want to make it up to you this weekend."

"Ok. I'd like that," she said grinning. "I would talk longer, but I need to go."

"Ok. I'm in bit of a hurry myself. I will talk to you soon. I'll be in my new home by then, too. Talk to you later." And he hung up.

Jaylon opened the door, and said, "Come back in. We need

to start loading the vehicles."

She put several boxes in the back of the Escalade, and in her car. When she turned to go back inside, she saw a white car slow down as it passed by the house. It was the same one that had followed her in the past. Only this time she could have sworn Sargent Maly was riding in the passengers' seat.

Jaylon looked at her and then looked up the street. "What's wrong?"

"Nothing. Eventually, I'm going to get the license plate of that car and find out who it belongs to."

"What are you talking about?"

"Never mind," she said as she went back into the house.

The next morning, they left out and drove south-east into the country. Five minutes later, a huge stone house came into view. He drove around the loop driveway in front of the house and parked.

Jaylon began unpacking the back seat of her car, but she just stood there amazed, staring at the stone mansion. When he saw the look of awe on her face, he laughed and said, "Yes this is my house. Close your mouth and grab some boxes, goofy."

He toted several boxes as he walked to the front door. He then propped his knee under them and opened it.

"Wow! This room is like mammoth," she said as they walked inside.

Her eyes followed the tall white walls and around to a baby grand piano that set to her left. Something about it seemed familiar. And right then Kohl walked into the room.

They stood in place grinning at each other while Jaylon babbled as he made his way through the room. When he realized that Renee was not behind him, he stopped and turned. He looked at Renee and then at Kohl. He cleared his throat, and said, "Kohl, this is my, or rather our housekeeper, Renee. Renee, this is my brother, Kohl."

Kohl's eyes widened. "She's your housekeeper?"

"He's your brother?" Renee replied shocked.

Jaylon kept quiet as things begun to sink in. "Well, it's about time I get to meet the mystery man," he said, with a sarcastic chuckle. He didn't know what to think about the two of them seeing each other, but jealousy sure wasn't running through his mind. He wasn't about to let the fact that she was seeing his brother bother him. Not one bit.

Kohl helped Renee set the boxes down. "You..." He couldn't think of anything else to say and embraced her.

Several seconds later, they heard, "Renee tell that man you are busy."

"I don't want to keep your boss waiting," Kohl said, with a smirk on his face.

She laughed. "And I sure don't want to test his patients right now. See you later."

The rest of the week was spent moving. A couple of the guys in the band and a few other friends helped move the furniture into the house. Jaylon wanted to hire a moving company, but his friends insisted they wanted to help. So, besides Kohl's things, the last thing to do was to make sure nothing was left in the former house.

The following day, Jaylon wasted no time going through what was now no longer his home. He headed upstairs and stood in the doorway of his old bedroom. He held back tears as he walked to the center of the room. "I miss you so, so much, Leaighanna," he said, and he went downstairs.

Renee came from the back room when she heard him say Leighanna's name. She walked up beside him and put her arm around his waist. "Hi. You going to be ok?"

He gave her a cold look and walked outside, leaving the front door open. When he didn't hear the door shut, he turned and saw her standing in the threshold.

"What?" he asked, cold. "What's wrong?"

She didn't say anything, and he went back inside.

"Maybe I shouldn't be moving into the new house. I'm seeing your brother, and you missing your wife, and all. It's just not the best thing for me to be doing."

He sighed hard and ran his hand through his hair. "Wait a second, I asked you to move to the new house because I wanted you to, and you know that. Yes, Leighanna and I made a lot of memories here, but there are new ones to be made, and she will be with the kids and me at the new house, as well. And honestly, I think your family, whom you won't talk about, will be with you."

"You have your precious memories and your kids," she said, upset. "All I have are precious memories."

He softened his mood and said, "You made me realize that just because someone dies don't mean they leave. That person is still very much part of you and always will be. Now, let's get out of here."

He locked the door and took one last look at the house before leaving.

Nothing was said between them until he stopped at the last stop light that led into the country. "So, you like Kohl?" he asked.

"I guess so," she said, grinning.

"You guess so?" He laughed, and then he thought about the night they shared and wondered if she had told Kohl. But he most certainly wasn't going to tell him.

Jaylon parked in the side driveway behind Stokie's truck.

"Hi. What a surprise," Jaylon said as they walked into the kitchen. Ryan, Shane, and a few members of the band were there. They had helped Kohl move his furniture into his living area of the house.

Renee walked down the side hallway that led to the front

room and stairway. And as she started to go upstairs, she heard Kohl playing the piano. Right then she got an idea and went back to the kitchen.

Jaylon and the rest of the company had gone outside, except for Stokie, who was getting a coke from the fridge.

She got a glass from the cabinet, took a twenty-dollar bill from her purse, and put it in the glass.

"Here," she said to Stokie. "Take this to the piano player."

Stokie chuckled. "Ok."

She then went back down the hallway, to the front room, and peaked around the corner only to see a young girl sitting beside Kohl. He sang out a few lyrics, and the girl laughed as he joked with her. Renee's heart began to race, wondering who the girl was, and why she was sitting next to him.

Stokie set the glass on the table. "This is from a lovely lady," he said, and he left.

Renee made an about-face turn when Kohl caught a glimpse of her. "Tyler, I need to go see the lovely lady."

"Ok. I'm going to go see what Dyllon and Reighanna are up to."

He knocked on Renee's bedroom door and walked in. She was standing on the balcony, and he walked up behind her and embraced her. "I've never had anyone give me a tip for playing the piano."

She turned and looked up at him. "Oh, really," she said, in an accusing way. "Not even the pretty young thing that was sitting next to you?"

He tried not to laugh knowing she was upset. "Dyllon's girlfriend likes to poke fun at my singing."

"Dyllon's girlfri . . . Oh." This time he couldn't help but laugh. "Maybe I can take you to find some furniture to set out here. We might want something to sit on."

"We. I like the sound of that."

"Me too." He slipped the twenty- dollar bill in the back pocket of her jeans. "You and I."

Chapter Twenty-one

On the far most northern edge of Queens Shores lies Tiar Boulevard. If you are in the mood for endless shopping, then Tiar Boulevard is the place to be. And after two months of constant cleaning and rearranging furniture, Renee was in a desperate need of a break.

"Hey Renee, look at this," Kohl said, for the umpteenth time.

"Hang on a second," she replied while looking at something else.

Kohl loved rare pieces of artwork, and he had an eye for certain styles of vintage clothing, but what sat before him was a vase that looked to be from the early forties. He was excited to find such a piece, even if it really wasn't from the forties.

"You know the table where special items that grandma and grandpa have given me over the years set?" he asked. "This would be perfect sitting in the center of them."

She smiled and placed her hand on his back. "I think so, too."

Several stores up Kohl saw a sheer purple blouse hanging inside a boutique window. "That would look great on you." She liked it, as well. "Come on. I want to buy it for you."

A little later, she got a few windows ahead of him, and she stopped dead in her tracks staring at a clear-cut princess diamond ring. "That is gorgeous" she muttered under her breath.

Kohl walked up behind her and put his arm around her waist. "Yes, it is. Go try it on."

She was so into the ring that she didn't realize he was talking to her.

He rubbed her back to get her attention. "Go try it on."

"Go try it on? Why?" she asked, baffled. "That's a special kind of ring. You know, the kind of ring that eventually takes you down an aisle to say I do. No."

"You mean you wouldn't marry me if I asked you to?" he asked, just to see what kind of reaction he would get from her. Her face blushed, unsure of how to answer him. "Come on. Just try it on for fun," he said.

"I saw the two of you looking at it," the jeweler said with a slight English accent. "It is a very nice ring. What size do you wear?"

Still baffled, she said, "Six, or a six and a half."

He got out both sizes.

"Let me," Kohl said. He held her left hand and slid the size six ring on the fourth finger. He smiled. "Gorgeous. This ring was made just for you."

She moved her hand through the light watching the diamond sparkle. "Yeah," she said, and then took it off.

"Thank you for showing us the ring," Kohl said to the jeweler.

"You are very welcome," he said as he handed Kohl his card.

Later that night, they sat on her balcony snuggling in one of the bamboo chairs Kohl bought for her. And in the quietness, he softly said, "That ring looked so pretty on your finger. I believe it was made just for you."

She looked into his eyes and smiled. "So, I've heard."

The next morning Renee followed the aroma of fresh coffee brewing in the kitchen.

Grandma grabbed two mugs, filled them to the brim, and set them on the island, and said, "Why are you up so early?"

"When did you get here?" Renee asked.

Grandma chuckled. "I was staying at Dave and Natalie's house because my air conditioner needs repairing. And wouldn't you know it, their air conditioner stopped working last night. You never answered my question. Why are you up so early on a Sunday morning? Church starts at eleven thirty, not seven."

Church? she thought, and then said, "I never heard you guys come in last night."

Grandma picked up her mug, took a sip, and gave her a curious smile.

"What?" Renee asked.

"Kohl really likes you. He talks to me about things he wouldn't talk about with others, and he talks about you, a lot. Kohl has not dated in years. He concentrated on his schooling, and on occasion, he would go on a date." She gave a quick chuckle. "Every time he would come home from a date, he would say, 'I hate dating. Remind me of that next time I get the idea to go on another one'. And then, of course, I would tell him that he is a special man, and someday a very special lady will walk right into his life, and he will be the happiest man alive." She took another sip of coffee. "And I believe you are that lady. I have never seen him as happy as he is now."

"Grandma, I am curious about something. I have heard

very little, if any, talk about grandpa."

Grandma got the coffee pot and refilled their mugs. "I would have thought Kohl had told you about him by now. Grandpa Earl died five years ago from a massive heart attack. Kohl was devastated. He and Kohl were best buddies. Jaylon and grandpa were close, as well, but there was a special bond between Kohl and grandpa. You would have loved him, and he would have thought the world of you, too," she said, smiling. "Now, how about fixing those amazing cinnamon rolls that Jaylon has bragged about for breakfast. Then you can go to church with us."

Talk about timing. Church, her faith, and being Christian, made for conversations with only a few certain people. Besides, she couldn't share her faith. She figured that people would just see the addict in her and think otherwise.

"Kohl told me you were from upstate New York. I bet you miss your family there," grandma said as Renee prepared the yeast dough. "Do you have children?"

Renee stopped kneading the dough and looked at her. She wasn't sure how to answer her question. She wasn't going to talk about her kids, not until she had a chance to speak with Kohl about them first.

"Well, Rick and Rachael Nolan became my legal guardians when I was a child. Rick was my doctor, and pain specialist, as well. When I turned eighteen, I changed my last name to Nolan. I talk to them on occasion. Though, I have not told them about the drugs and all. Just haven't had the chance."

Grandma put her arm around her shoulder, and said, "It's good you still talk to them, even though it isn't as often as you would like."

A few hours later, Kohl walked into the kitchen grinning. "I smell cinnamon." He put his arm around Renee. "Did you make them?"

117

"Not just me. A beautiful lady, whom you get your looks from, helped."

"Did you sleep well?" he asked.

Jaylon came around the corner from the hallway, yawning, and said. "I'm sure his new California King memory foam mattress is very comfortable."

"Jaylon, you're nosing in something that is none of your business," grandma said.

"I wouldn't know about his bed," Renee smarted back at him.

"You mean you two haven't-," Jaylon joked.

"No, we haven't," Kohl said before Jaylon could say anything else.

"Haven't what?" Dave asked as he and Natalie joined them.

Grandma chimed in just in time. "You two are going to church with Dave, Natalie, and I. And Jaylon, you and the kids are going, as well."

Kohl grinned. Good save, grandma, he thought.

Chapter Twenty-two

When Renee was a child her biological father had this saying, Sunday go to meet'n. He was talking about church, and that phrase has stuck in the back of her mind ever since, and especially now.

Kohl stood at the bottom of the stairs talking to Jaylon and unaware that Renee was watching him from the top of the stairs.

Kohl sported jeans and casual black shirt, and his hair lay in messy curls, just the way she liked it. She then went to take another look in the mirror at what she was wearing.

Kohl peered around the corner of the bathroom. "You wear the blouse well. I'm glad I bought it for you," he said, jokingly. "Come on. We're riding with Jaylon."

After a fifteen-minute ride through the country, a sign on top of a small building came into view that read, CHURCH. Talk about keeping it simple, she thought.

Pastor Benny, or Benny as he likes to be called, greeted everyone from the podium. Benny was of medium stature, brown hair, and sported a casual jacket and jeans. He, also, was holding an iPad instead of a bible.

Kohl led Renee to the front where Dave and Natalie sat. And as she listened to the sermon, she felt God's presence surrounding her. And right then, a wild thought came to mind.

She leaned toward Dave, and whispered, "Please tell me there isn't a bucket of rattlesnakes you all are going to dance around later testing God."

Kohl heard what she said, and he pressed his lips together to keep from laughing out loud.

Dave gave a quiet chuckle, and whispered, "Benny saves that for the evening service."

When the sermon had ended, Benny walked over to Kohl and Renee. "Been awhile, Kohl. Work finally let you out," he said while shaking his hand. "It's nice to see the two of you here. I hope to see you more often." He smiled. "And your brother, as well."

"You probably will," Kohl said. "I've missed worshiping with fellow Christians."

"Good. I'll see you later this evening."

"Evening?" Renee said, curious.

"Yes. Grandma invited me over for supper," Benny said to her.

Kohl grinned knowing what was going through her mind. "I think Jaylon is waiting for us." And as they walked out of the church, he laughed, "You have a wild imagination. Snakes."

"It was just a thought that went through my mind," she said, with a slight smile.

Later that evening, Renee went for a stroll around the property. She inhaled the fresh air and enjoyed the silence and thinking about church. She liked how Benny led the sermon. He was more of a teacher, and that was a huge plus.

When she turned to go back, she noticed the side door, near the kitchen door, was open. So, she went inside.

Jaylon said he wanted a state of the art studio, and he wasn't kidding. "This is fantastic," she said. He had a huge grin on his face. "You had that same grin the first time I saw the glass frame of your platinum albums and CDs. Oh, and an Egyptian carpet," she said, even more impressed.

"Pretty fine, ain't it."

She laughed. He was like a kid a Christmas only having many Christmases at one time.

"Are you going for a run?" he asked, seeing that she was wearing a new pair of running shoes.

"No. Just came in from a short walk around the lawn. I'm going back inside. Congrats. You deserve all of this."

Chapter Twenty-three

Autumn was officially here, and the mountains were in a full-color scheme. Back east was pretty this time of year as well, but even more so in Queens Shores. Then again, being in love with a gorgeous man might have something to do with her opinion.

Kohl realized just how much he missed worshiping with other church members, so he and Renee started attending church regularly. He told Renee that the peace she had been feeling was God working in her life. And every day, before he left for work, he would tell her to let God have her past, her hurts, and her addictions, every second of the day, and then he would pray with her.

On another note, Jaylon's recording studio was finished. He had a passion for working with new artists, and bands, and especially the local talent. His band was given a chance by a top recording artist and producer, and this was his way of giving back. And at this point in his life, this was better than being on tour.

One afternoon, Jaylon and Stokie were working on a couple of tracks when Kohl walked in, checking the studio out.

"Wow," Kohl sort of chuckled. "This was worth leaving work early for. You need a few more gold and platinum albums, and CD's on the wall," he said, sarcastic.

Stokie laughed.

Jaylon cleared his throat. "You know you don't have to leave work just to come here."

"Actually, I have another reason for coming home early, and I plan on taking her out."

"Aint love grand," Stokie joked.

At that comment, Jaylon changed the subject back to the track they were working on.

In the meantime, Renee sat at the family computer desk, uploading pictures of her children from her laptop onto a CD. Pictures from newborn, and to the age they were last time she saw them, laying in their bed sound asleep with no clue they would never wake up again.

When she finished, she took the disk from the drive and wrote 'Once' on the face of it. She placed the CD in the clear plastic jacket and set it on the desk. Tears slipped from the corners of her eyes and ran down her cheeks falling onto the jacket. This is one pain that nothing could take away, and only one thing could numb it, even if it were just for a little while.

Immediately, she dashed upstairs and stood in the middle of her room, wanting to numb those memories. And then she remembered, in the back corner of her closet was a box of odds and ends and just maybe something else.

"Jackpot," she muttered, upon opening the box.

Unmoving, she stared at the tapped-up bundle as she held in her hand. She then threw it back into the box and then took it out. Oh, how she wanted to feel the needle hitting her vein, and the warmth spreading throughout her body, melting the pain away.

Her hands shook so hard that she thought she wasn't going to be able to open it. And then just like that, the contents fell onto the floor. Everything she needed was right in front of her. She stared at the small amount of heroin. It was just enough to get the job done, and maybe even twice.

In the meantime, Kohl walked into the family room and noticed Renee's was laptop sitting on the computer desk, and it was open. He went over to it and picked up the CD.

"Once," he muttered. He then took it upstairs where he hoped to find Renee.

Renee slid the needle into her vein, when she heard, "No!" you are not doing this," Kohl said, trying to get the syringe from her.

"You don't understand."

"Then help me to understand," he pleaded.

"Nobody can help me, Kohl. I couldn't open up to Ryan about certain things. And I'm not going to burden you, or anyone else, with my past. Now, get out!"

"No! You are not going to drown your sorrow in heroin. Now take the needle out of your arm."

She ignored him and tried to inject the dope, but her hands shook so erratically that she couldn't hold the syringe steady. "I can't do this," she said, livid, and took the needle out.

Immediately, he yanked the syringe from her hand and threw it across the room, and said, "I want the rest of it."

Reluctantly, she handed him what was left of the heroin only to try and take it back.

"Renee. You are not doing this," he said, stern, "and I know you really don't want to, either."

He snatched the dope from her hand and flushed it down the toilet. He then smashed the syringe with his foot and threw it away. "Come on. Let's go sit on the balcony."

As they cuddled in one of the bamboo chairs, he said, "I'm sorry about what happened in New York. I wish you talk to me about it, but using dope isn't the way to deal with it. Have you read the book that Ryan gave you? The one with the bible verses in it."

She didn't reply. In fact, she didn't say anything until the clear blue sky faded to a purple and marigold hue.

"I love when the evening sky paints itself in my favorite colors." She turned and looked at him. "I want to show you what's on the CD."

"How about we go to Maury's and look at it there," he said.

A half hour later, they sat down in a booth near the back of the diner only for her to notice Detective Leary and Sargent Maly sitting at the counter.

Detective Leary nodded hello to her.

"What can I get for you," a waitress asked her and Kohl.

"Would you like something to eat or just coffee?" Kohl asked Renee.

"Just coffee, please."

The waitress took their order and left.

Sargent Maly looked over at Kohl. "If I'm thinking right that's Jaylon MacKie's brother."

Detective Leary got up and went over to their table, and Sargent Maly followed him.

"Hello, Renee," he said.

Kohl looked at the two of them wondering how they knew her.

"This is Kohl," Renee said to them.

"You're Jaylon's brother, right?" Sargent Maly asked.

Kohl kept quiet.

"I don't mean to interrupt," Detective Leary said. "I just want to let you know that I'm still working on your family's case. I think we may have a few new leads that look very hopeful."

Just great, she thought. Now she had to explain to Kohl what they were talking about. "That's great. I appreciate you telling me."

As he turned to leave, he said, "Nice to meet you, Kohl. She's a very nice lady."

As he walked away, Sargent Maly gave Renee a hard glance and then went back to the counter where they were sitting.

"What was that look about?" Kohl asked.

"He has no reason to look at me that way. He doesn't even know me." Right then, she remembered thinking that it was him she saw in the white car the day her and Jaylon were moving.

"Um, so just how do you know them?"

"I left New York to start over and wouldn't you know it, it followed me up here. Detective Leary is working on the case of my family's murder. Let's get out here. We can look at the CD at home."

As they got into the car, he said, "Thought we would take a ride before heading home."

He made a right turn at the park, cruised by the bay, and then pulled up along the curb, and shifted into park. "So, when the detective mentioned your family, did he mean mom, dad, brother, and sister, kind of family, or did he mean husband, kids, and four-legged critters?"

She laughed. "The later, minus the critters. My family, they are in heaven. One of the two that murdered them is in prison for life, and Detective Leary is looking for the other one. I'd just like to know what he is doing to find this person."

Feeling relieved, he said, "It's pretty amazing how they can find someone when all they have are a few leads." He held her hand and kissed it. "I am so sorry about your family, but I still would like to see the CD."

"Thank you. I'm glad you understand." But right now, Sargent Maly was more on her mind than looking at the CD.

Chapter Twenty-four

A few weeks later, Jaylon took a break from the studio to work on the building on the back lawn. The wood floor in the main room needed to be sanded and stained, and the lights needed to be updated, and he wanted it finished before the holidays.

In the meantime, Kohl kept busy cooking. He was working on a special vegetable soup recipe for the family Thanksgiving meal, and it had to be perfect. Especially since his uncle Kerry and his family were coming up from the southern part of Oregon.

A few days before Thanksgiving, Kohl strolled into the kitchen while talking on his phone. Dave, Natalie, and Jaylon were sitting at the island eating an early lunch. They knew he was up to something big by the giddy smile on his face.

He pressed the end call button, and said, "If Renee wakes up tell her I had to go the hospital, and I'll be back later."

"Sure thing," Dave said. "But I have a feeling you are going somewhere other than the hospital."

Kohl grabbed his coat off the hook by the door. "Come on Jaylon," he said, anxious. "I want to leave before she wakes up."

Jaylon picked his coffee mug up. Kohl gave him a what are you doing kind of look. "If I'm going, then so is my coffee. I won't spill it in your precious car," Jaylon said.

"You're the same way about your Jaguar," Kohl said, laughing under his breath.

"Hey, don't forget that your uncle Kerry and his family will be here in a little while," Dave said.

"We're not going to be gone the whole day," Kohl said as they walked out the door.

A half-hour later Kohl parked in front of Tiar Jewelers. Jaylon grinned. He now understood why Kohl was in such a hurry. Pure excitement.

"Mr. MacKie, right," the jeweler said as they walked in.

Kohl nodded yes.

"I have your rings right here."

Kohl held the diamond ring into the light and smiled. "You should have seen this on her finger. She didn't say much about it, but I could tell she loved it because of the way she waved her hand in the light just to see it sparkle. I have told her many times this ring was made for her."

"I couldn't agree more," the jeweler said. "And your matching ring is very handsome, as well."

Kohl tried it on to make sure it fit. "Did you ever think you would see me wearing a wedding ring?" he said to Jaylon.

"She hasn't said yes, yet," Jaylon said with sarcasm, but Kohl ignored him.

"Very nice, Mr. MacKie," the jeweler said as Kohl handed it back to him. "And her diamond ring is a size six," he said, checking it again, "And her wedding band is a size six, as well."

"That's right. Thank you for holding these for me."

He smiled, and said, "My pleasure. I knew you would be back."

As they left the store, Jaylon chuckled at Kohl. He was excited for him, even though he couldn't help but be a little jealous.

"I want this to be a surprise," Kohl said, as he drove home. He was so ecstatic about the rings that he didn't realize he was heading in the wrong direction. "She is not big on formal weddings, or big to-do's, so I want to ask her to marry me when she least expects it. I haven't even told her that I love her, yet."

"You haven't told her that you love her, yet? And you bought wedding rings?" Jaylon said, baffled, but Kohl didn't reply. Right then Jaylon got an idea. The building on the back lawn was the perfect place for a surprise wedding. He then laughed out loud.

"What?" Kohl asked.

"Well, unless you are going to Seattle, I suggest you turn around and head south."

"What do you mean?" He then saw the sign that read, 'Seattle - 150 Miles'. "Oh, good grief," Kohl said, aggravated.

"Good grief is right. You're definitely in love. By the way, I want to stop by the lumber store before going home. I need stain for the floors in the back building."

"You should start your own carpentry business," Kohl quipped.

"Ha. It's just a hobby."

In the meantime, Natalie and Renee made a trip to Laurens Bakery to pick up an order.

While Natalie talked with Lauren, Renee browsed through the cake section.

Moments later, Natalie noticed Renee eyeing a particular

cake.

"What a perfect cake," Renee said to her. Soft coral frosting, detailed latticework, and pearls embellished it. "If I were to get married again, this would be the kind of cake I would want," she said, not realizing what she had just said.

Natalie grinned. "Come on. I think Lauren has my order ready."

On the drive back home, Natalie said, "I'm so excited that Dave's family is coming up. I just wish my sister and her husband were able to come up, as well. That would make everything perfect."

Natalie came to the road that leads to their home and stopped. And, at the same time, Kohl and Jaylon passed by in front of them.

"What are they doing?" Renee asked. "I thought Kohl had to go to the hospital."

"It's hard telling what they are up to," Natalie said, not knowing what else to say.

When she pulled into the driveway and parked, she saw that there was another car behind Jaylon's Escalade.

"My sister is here!" Natalie said. And she hurried inside the house.

Kohl and Jaylon came over to help carry the pastry boxes inside the house. "Hi. Sorry I wasn't here when you woke up. I needed to..." and then he paused, knowing he almost told on himself. "I had something I needed to take care of, and Jaylon needed stain for the building on the back lawn. Everything go ok with you and mom?"

She didn't answer. She was watching Natalie hugging her sister, through the kitchen window.

"Renee?"

She half smiled. "It's rather sweet. I mean, your whole family is all about love."

Kohl kissed her on the cheek. "Yes, we are, and you're are part of us, too." He chuckled. "So, smile bigger, goofy."

The following Thursday, the kitchen was in full motion. As the turkey baked in the oven, Kohl prepared his soup, grandma peeled the potatoes, and Renee kneaded yeast dough while Natalie unloaded the dishwasher.

Renee set the dough next to the oven to rise. She then grabbed an armload of plates and took them to the dining room.

"Sure is noisy in there," Jaylon said as he came from the family room.

Natalie looked at him as if to say be quiet.

Jaylon hugged her and kissed her on the cheek. "You know I'm kidding. I'm glad they are here," he said, trying to keep the sarcasm from showing.

"Good save, Jaylon," she chuckled. She knew Jaylon loved having both sides of the family here, but he was never keen on a lot of people being in the house and all the noise that tends to go with it.

Renee returned for more plates, but no sooner than she left the kitchen, Kohl hollered, "Wait a second. Come back here."

She made an about-face turn and stood in the doorway. "What?"

"Come here."

She rolled her eyes and walked over to him. "I need to set the table," she said as she set the plates on the counter.

He set the spoon down and took her into his arms and kissed her. "I love you."

She had waited so long to hear him say those three words, yet she just stood there shaking her head like a bobblehead doll, and grinning. She then gave him a quick kiss, picked the plates up, and left the room.

Jaylon, Natalie, and grandma just stood there staring at

him. Grandma chimed in with a heavy sigh, "Well, what took you so long? I thought you would never tell her that."

"Perfect timing, grandma," Kohl said. "Perfect timing."

"He's what you call a slow cooker," Jaylon said.

Natalie couldn't help but laugh as she remembered telling Jaylon that he about missed out on having freshly baked bread the day he had interviewed Renee.

And a few hours later, the whole family sat at the dining room table, set for a feast on this Thanksgiving evening. Dave said a short prayer of thanks, and his brother, Kerry, chimed in with a bold, "Amen."

Later that night, Kohl and Renee went outside for some fresh air. The wind picked up, swirling bits of glistening snow around them, and he pulled her close to him to help break the chill.

"I meant what I said," Kohl said.

She ran her fingers through his tousled curls that were now coated with snow. "I-I love you. I love you." There. She had finally said those three words that she thought she could never say to another man.

"You don't know how good those words sound coming from you. I love you, Renee.

Chapter Twenty-five
November

Christmas would soon be approaching, and Natalie wanted to get a jump start on shopping. Not wanting to go alone, she invited Renee to go with her to an outside mall south of Queens Shores.

Renee trailed behind Natalie as they went from one store to another. And every so often, she would glance at the price tags of certain items, raise her eyebrows, and quickly move on.

Mick's Boutique was the last store on the strip. Renee stopped and gazed at a pair of sandals that would add six inches to her height. Leather straps wrapped around the ankle and purple and gold beads embellished the toe of the sexy stiletto.

"Go try them on," Natalie said.

"I don't think wearing those while cleaning house would be a good thing," she said, with sarcasm.

"Kohl wouldn't mind."

"Ok," Renee giggled.

"You know what I meant. Come on. You're going to go try them on."

"This is a very pretty and delicate sandal," the clerk said, putting them on her feet.

"Ok. Now what?" Renee said. "I mean, they are exceptionally nice. More like WOW nice."

"Walk in them," Natalie coaxed.

"How much are they?" Renee asked as she walked around the boutique.

The clerk told her five hundred and fifty dollars. Off they came faster than a blink of an eye.

"What are you doing?" Natalie asked.

"That is way too much money for shoes. That's part of a house payment, groceries..." and she stopped talking, seeing the confused look on Natalie's face.

"I want to buy them for you."

"No. No. There is no way I can wear shoes that cost this much, nor would I feel right if you spent that kind of money on me."

Renee thanked the clerk, and they left the boutique.

"I think we have walked the entire mall, or so say my aching feet," Natalie said. "Let's go home."

"I think we have, too. Besides I don't think our hands can manage any more bags."

Natalie pulled into the driveway and parked behind Kohl's car. "Kohl would have liked to see you wearing those sandals."

"Natalie, I appreciate you wanting to buy them for me. I just know what it's like to be dirt broke." She gave a small shrug. "Yet, I spent money on dope, but unlike in New York, I had money. Not that having money made it right. Doesn't matter if you're rich or poor. Never mind. I'm really sorry."

Natalie touched her shoulder. "It's ok. We had a good time."

"Yes, we did," Renee said, grinning.

Later that same week, on Saturday afternoon, Kohl was taking Renee out for the day. She wore black jeans and the purple blouse he had bought her, and he wore skinny black jeans and a white silk blouse.

And just as they were leaving, Natalie text Kohl. "I'll be right back. Mom needs me for a second," he said to her.

He went to the den where his mom was. "Hey. What's up?" he asked her, with a curious grin on his face.

She opened a Mick's Boutique shoe box. "Renee saw these while we were out shopping the other night. I got her to try them on, and she loved them, but-"

"She wouldn't let you buy them for her," Kohl said, chuckling.

"Yes, because she said they cost too much. So, I went back and bought them for her, and I want you to give them to her."

"Thanks, mom," he said and kissed her on the cheek.

He slipped out the back door, put them in the trunk of his car, and went back inside.

"Ok. Let's go have some fun," Kohl said to Renee.

After a late afternoon spent at Tiar Boulevard, he drove downtown and parked in front of Tara's Hair Studio and Spa.

"What are we doing here?" Renee asked him.

"There is someone I want you to meet," he said as they got out of the car.

A lady with long dark hair greeted them as they walked inside. "Hello, Kohl," she said, excited to see the two of them.

"Hi, Tara. This is my lady, Renee."

"So, this is who you have mentioned to me many times. The last few times he's been in for a haircut, he has talked about you nonstop. Follow me," she said.

"You still haven't told me what we are doing?" Renee whispered to Kohl.

He shrugged his shoulders, and they followed Tara to a room where manicure tables lined one wall, and pedicure spas lined the opposite wall.

"Have a seat at the purple foot spa. Take your shoes and socks off while I go find a chair for Kohl."

Seconds later she set a chair next to her and Renee. "Kohl told me that he wanted to bring you here to be spoiled. So just relax. Zola will be in shortly to polish your fingernails."

Renee sort of laughed, and he shrugged his shoulders, again, as he sat down in the chair.

And an hour later, Renee's toenails, and fingernails shone with a dazzling purple glaze.

"That certain ring would look stunning on your finger," Kohl said.

Renee grinned. "Yes, it would."

He cleared his throat, and said, "I need to go out to the car for a second."

A few moments later he returned, holding his left arm behind his back. "Close your eyes."

Renee chuckled. "What are you up to?"

"Just close your eyes and keep them shut," he said.

Tara quickly got up, so he could sit in front of Renee.

He gently held her foot, slid a sandal on one foot, and did the same with the other foot. "There. Now you can open your eyes."

Her eyes widened in awe. On her feet were the sandals, the five hundred and fifty-dollar sandals, that Natalie wanted to buy her. She started to speak, when he said, "Mom bought them for you. She wanted you to have them."

"Wow," she said excitedly, as she walked around the room in them.

Kohl took out his credit card to pay Tara and Zola.

"No. No. This ones on me," Tara said.

"Thank you," he said, handing them each a fifty-dollar bill.

"You had this all planned, didn't you?" Renee said as they left.

He opened the car door for her and kissed her. When he got behind the wheel, he whispered a sweet nothing in her ear.

She laughed. "I never knew a pair of shoes could make a man... Your mom said you would like them."

He sighed, "Yeah."

By the time they arrived home, the black sky shimmered in a blanket of stars, and they had company. A lot of company. Their driveway was full, so he pulled up along the side of his bedroom and parked.

"I'm eventually going have my own driveway and an entry door put in," he said as they got out of the car. "I didn't know there was a party tonight."

"Me either," Renee said as they approached the building on the back lawn.

Music filtered through the speakers, and food was laid out on the counter, while close friends and family dinned at the tables that was situated in a half circle.

"It's about time you two arrived," Dyllon said.

"I'm starved. Let's eat," Kohl said.

They filled their plates and went over to Natalie, Dave, and grandma's table.

"You're somewhat taller than I remember," Dave said.

Natalie chuckled as Renee mouthed a thank you to her. But no sooner than they got seated, Jaylon came over and nudged Kohl on the shoulder.

"I'll be back," Kohl said.

He followed Jaylon to the back of the room, and said, "What's up?"

"So," Jaylon smiled, "you said you wanted to marry Renee when she least expected it. How about right now?"

"This is this perfect time," Kohl said, excited. "But what about the rings and marriage license. Wait, you had all of this planned." And he joked, "She hasn't said yes, yet."

Jaylon laughed knowing he was referring to the comment he made when Kohl bought the rings. "I don't think she is going to turn you down. Now go tell Dyllon to get the rings, and that will give you a chance to talk to Renee."

Kohl told Dyllon where the rings were at, and then he went over to Renee and whispered in her ear, "Come with me for a second."

Seeing how anxious he was, she knew something had to be wrong. "What? What's wrong?" she asked, worried.

"Nothing," He cleared his throat and said, "Will you marry me? Tonight? Like, right now."

"Yes!"

"Jaylon had planned this party for us, so everything has been taken care of."

Jaylon stood near the area where he and Stokie were going to sing a few songs while keeping an eye on Kohl and Renee.

Kohl turned, looked at Jaylon, and grinned.

"There's going to be a wedding tonight," Jaylon announced, excited.

Benny stood behind a table at the front of the room, and a bible and a white candle was centered on it. Kohl asked Jaylon to be his best man, and Renee gestured at Reighanna to be her maid of honor.

"What about the rings? We don't have any," Renee said.

Benny took the rings from Dyllon and set them in front of the candle. Renee gleamed. It was the diamond ring Kohl had her try on, along with two matching wedding bands.

Kohl picked up the diamond ring, held her left hand, and slid it on her fourth finger. "We are now engaged."

Benny said a short prayer, and then recited 1st Corinthians

13:4-8. Kohl and Renee said their own short vows, which included their first date at the hospital cafeteria, and they sealed them with a rather long kiss.

"It is my pleasure to introduce Mr. and Mrs. Kohl and Renee MacKie," Benny announced.

As claps and clinks on stemware filled the room, Reighanna noticed the slight look of regret in her dad's eyes. She knew he still had feelings for Renee. In fact, she knew from the moment she met Renee last Christmas that he loved her. She now wondered why they never got past being close friends.

Moments later Natalie and grandma came from the kitchen carrying the frosted coral cake Renee saw at the bakery. Lauren had intertwined lattice work around the pearls and graced the top with beautiful flowers.

"Compliments of Laurens Bakery," Natalie said to Renee.

While everyone was enjoying the cake, Stokie picked up his guitar, and Jaylon took to the microphone.

"I wrote this song for a special person, my wife," Jaylon said, getting everyone's attention. "I rewrote some of the lyrics for a special couple, hoping they would dance to it tonight."

The lights dimmed as two spotlights lit the center of the room.

"Guess that's our cue," Kohl said.

He led Renee under the light and slowly spun her around. She leaned her head against Kohl's chest as Jaylon begun to sing, and then she laughed. She had never been tall enough for her head to touch the top of his top chest. Kohl then placed his hand on the back of her head and touched her lips with his.

Several hours later, when the reception had settled down, they thanked everyone, and especially Jaylon, for tonight. Jaylon then took out an envelope from his jacket and handed it to them. He, Dave, Natalie, and grandma, had booked them a three-night stay at West Bay's luxury hotel wedding suite.

Kohl and Renee didn't leave the hotel until the fourth day. And as they drove out of the parking garage, Ricky was in the area and spotted them. He followed them from a distance until Kohl stopped at a traffic light, so he pulled over and waited for the light to change to green.

"There you are, my sweet Renee. I've been thinking about you," Ricky said to himself. Ricky had kept a low profile for several months. The police had stepped up their watch on the local drug scene, and he knew they were closer to finding the leader of the drug cartel.

When the traffic light turned green, he continued to follow them from a distance as they drove out of the city. "Moved to the country, did you?" He saw the right turn signal on Kohls car blinking, so he slowed down and waited for him to turn.

Kohl glanced in the rear-view mirror, and he realized that a car had been following them since they left the hotel. But he gave it no thought, thinking that it was just someone else who lived in the area.

After Kohl turned on to their road, Ricky proceeded. And a few moments later, he came upon a stone mansion. "That's it. Has to be their house." He saw the tail lights on Kohl's car flash off, and Jaylon's Escalade parked in front of it. "But she likes red cars, Kohl. Not black. You have done well my sweet Renee. We will see how long this will last."

As they walked to the house, Kohl noticed Ricky looking their way as he drove by.

Jaylon sat at the kitchen island reading the local paper. "Did you two have a good time?" he asked them.

"Yes, we did," Renee said. "So much so that we didn't leave the hotel."

Jaylon glanced at her trying not to show any kind of emotion. "That's nice."

"Just some FYI here, Jaylon," Kohl said. "You might want

to get some outdoor security cameras. You may have fans driving by hoping to get a look at you."

"Never had that problem before. Good idea, though. Glad you both had a great time," he said, keeping his eyes on the paper.

Chapter Twenty-six

Dave and Natalie didn't like the terrible direction their neighborhood was headed in, so they put their house up for sale. That is where Jaylon stepped in and told them they could occupy the west wing of his house. He would do whatever renovations they wanted to make his home feel like their home, as well. Kohl didn't mind, but Renee wasn't so sure about it. Then again, Dave had this saying, more love. Meaning, the more family that's around, then there's more love and happiness around. Renee always admired how everyone got along so well, and she just hoped it would stay that way.

In the meantime, Christmas was four weeks away. Kohl worked a lot during those few weeks before Christmas, and there were many times he would walk in the door only to get called back to the hospital. The only problem with him being gone so much was that Renee had to figure out ways to occupy her time. Especially when thoughts of using, and not using, and missing her kids, invaded every cell of her brain. And with

Christmas near, it only made things worse.

On one long afternoon, her thinking was in overdrive. Full throttle was more like it. Instead of getting upset, as the last time, she began to quote scripture and pray for strength. And within a few moments, she calmed down and went for a long walk hoping the fresh air would invigorate her.

Snow danced through the air and lightly touched the ground only for the wind to dust it away. By the time she reached an old library, the snow was sticking to the ground. She looked back at her footprints and smiled, as flashbacks of seeing her kid's footprints in the snow came to mind.

Bells on the door jingled as she walked inside the library. Christmas incense chased away the scent of old library books, and the wood floor creaked with each step she took. And as she walked down the aisles, another smile came across her face, remembering how her kids loved to visit the library. She then gathered an arm full of holiday books and magazines and checked them out.

An hour and a few more inches of snow later, she was back home sipping hot coffee while flipping through pages of the books and magazines.

Natalie, on the other hand, was in the dining room sorting through boxes of Christmas decorations. One thing the family knew not to do was to interfere with her decorating, but Renee couldn't help but overhear her complaining about not having enough time to decorate.

"Natalie, I would really like to help you," Renee said, walking over to her.

Natalie looked up from the boxes. "You know, I could use some help. There are a ten-foot tree and two six-foot trees to assemble, and the rest of the decorations to put up, as well.

The two of them worked until late evening, when Natalie

said, "I'm done for the evening. The rest can wait until tomorrow."

Renee didn't mind in the least. That gave her and Kohl just enough time to go to a nearby tree farm to cut a special tree for their bedroom.

The following evening, she stood at the front room window looking out at the fresh blanket of snow glittering under the moonlight. Vivid memories of her kids throwing snowballs, making snow angels, and a snowman, flashed through her mind. It was all so real that it was all she could do to keep from running outside and embracing them. "I miss you guys. I miss you so much," she muttered.

"It snowed," Kohl said, startling her as he wrapped his arms around her. "You're in deep thought."

She turned and snuggled against him. "Yeah. Just remembering things."

"Like what?"

"Every Christmas my daughter Chloe and I would go downtown to see the decorations and window shop. We always had a great time. My son Pauly loved the snow, as well." She paused. "I could have sworn he was looking right at me and laughing, just as he always did. He would try and catch snowflakes on his tongue, and the three of us would throw snowballs at each other."

"Well, they would really love living up here during the winter. Even though you have told me very little about your family, I still would like to see the CD." He then ran his hand through her hair and kissed her.

Christmas Eve night, Renee sat on the floor in front of their tree excited that it was their first Christmas together. Kohl joined her and set a tray in front of her. On it was a small red box, a red plate, a fork, and two Christmas mugs filled to the brim with hot chocolate and topped with whipped cream.

"Open the box," he said.

She was so excited that she nearly tore the lid off the box. "It's the top of our wedding cake."

"Tradition says you should wait till your first anniversary before eating the top of your wedding cake. But, I thought eating this together on this special night would bring back the light in your eyes that I haven't seen for a few days. I know this is a hard time for you, missing your kids and all."

"This is perfect."

Renee cut small piece with the fork and held it between her fingers. Kohl then wrapped his fingers around hers and took a bite. "Now it's perfect," he said.

The next morning, the delicious aroma of apples and cinnamon graced the air. Carols played in the background, and shiny ribbons peaked out from underneath the trees. Reighanna and Dyllon went around the tree gathering their gifts from Jaylon, while the rest of them passed out gifts to each other. And a Laurens Bakery breakfast and coffee sat on the coffee table.

When some of the excitement settled, Jaylon handed Renee a card with red, gold, and purple ribbons wrapped around it. It contained ten one-hundred-dollar bills, just like last year. She told him she would put in the bank with the money he had given her last year, and that she was just waiting for that something special to buy with it. He thought she had spent that money on heroin, so he was happy to know she still had it.

Later that night, as Kohl and Renee crawled into bed, he said, "Since we didn't get each other anything for Christmas, let's go on a shopping spree after New Year's."

"Sounds good to me, and you can buy me lots of things," she said teasingly.

On New Year's they went to Mike's Pub. Mike let them have all the food and drinks they wanted as a wedding gift from him and Carmen. Even though Kohl likes to have an occasional vodka drink, they only drank cokes.

They never did run into Ricky, which she thought was strange since this was his side of town. As far as that goes, she hasn't seen him since that awful night he left her dying in the bar, though she has seen that same white car at times. And, as usual, it would always slow down just enough to grab her attention and then speed on by.

The MacKie family, their friends, and Mike and Carmen were the only people she knew. But now she wondered if the car has something to do with the guy Detective Leary was looking for, especially since she saw Sargent Maly in the car the day her and Jaylon moved into the house.

Chapter Twenty-seven
One Year Later

Kohl and Renee celebrated their first wedding anniversary at the same hotel where they spent their honeymoon. And as the saying goes, time flies when you're having fun.

Sobriety looked good on Renee, and a few times a week she helped Ryan and Brenda at their rehab house, and the bad flare-ups of pain had not shown up since she and Kohl married. As for Kohl, he became a partner of Dr. Jo's practice. He even started taking extra classes to earn certification in the field of pain management.

In Renee's eyes everything was perfect, and every so often she would pause just to make sure she wasn't dreaming, especially about Kohl. She loved him more than life its self, and he loved her all the same. Nothing, or nobody, would ever dare to stand between their love for each other. Not even the questions that had been roaming through Reighanna's mind since she met Renee.

The following January, one late afternoon, Jaylon was going over some of his band's previous tracks. As far as he was concerned his studio was the best place to be on a blustery winter day. But his solitude was interrupted by a blast of bitterly cold air hitting him on the back.

Reighanna walked in, stomping the snow off her boots. "Hi, dad," she said, giddy. "Was that Renee I saw out running? The girl is crazy for being out in this weather."

Jaylon shivered and said, "Hurry up and shut the door."

She shut the door, took her boots off, set them next to the kitchen door, and then plopped down in the chair beside him.

"She wears the right clothing to run in this kind of weather, so she stays plenty warm. So, what brings you here?" he asked her. "Wait, don't answer just yet." He handed her his coffee mug. "Refill, please."

Reighanna was careful not to spill the coffee upon returning. So careful that she didn't realize the kitchen door didn't shut completely behind her.

In the meantime, Natalie came home from a long day of shopping. She set her bags on the kitchen island when she noticed the studio door was ajar. She wanted to say hi to Jaylon, but she thought he heard him talking on the phone. So, she hung her coat and hat on the hook in the hallway and then went back. Only this time she heard Reighanna talking to him.

"You really care about her, don't you?" Reighanna asked him.

"Who?" Jaylon said, bobbing his head to the beat of the music.

She giggled at him and then said. "Renee."

"Oh. I care about her a lot. I consider her one of my closest friends. Why? I don't think you came here to talk about her."

"Well, since we are on the subject of Renee, I have been

curious about something for a while now," she said as she twirled a few strands of hair between her fingers.

He took a sip of coffee wondering what was going through her mind, and then he turned the music down

"Do you have feelings for Renee?"

Natalie's eyes widened. She leaned in closer to the door thinking she misunderstood what she heard.

He about chocked and set the mug down. Just go for the jugular, he thought as he turned his attention back to the mixing board. "Why do you ask? And now of all times. She's married."

"I have always been curious. I don't know."

"Yes, you do know."

"You and Renee were so close. I know you had strong feelings for her before she met Kohl. You were so caring toward her like you were in love with her. Big time. And I saw the look of regret in your eyes on their wedding night. And every now and then, you still look at her that way."

"You have been thinking about this for over a year, and now of all times you suddenly pop this question on me?"

"I care for Renee, too, and especially Dyllon. He got attached to her like she was his mother."

"What do you really want to know? I mean, do you want to know if we dated?" She didn't answer and kept twirling her hair. "I took her out a few times. Not sure if I would call them dates, even though they could have passed for dates."

"Did you two ever," she hesitated as a curious teenage smile came across her face, "you know?"

Natalie swallowed hard, trying not to gasp at what Reighanna had just asked him.

"Did we ever what?" he asked while moving a few buttons on the mixing board. And then he realized just what she was asking. He sat back in his chair baffled about why she was bringing this up. He knew the question could come up at some point, but at the same time, he hoped it never would.

"That's a bold question to ask your father. What's it to you, anyway? It's not something you need to be concerned about."

"So, I'm right."

He didn't want to answer her. He would rather lie, but he taught his kids never to lie, and had a strict rule about it. Though everything inside him was telling him to do so, he couldn't.

"If I don't answer you, you will think Renee and I, as you put it, you knowed." He sighed hard and cleared his throat. "We shared a night, slept together, but we knew it wasn't right, so nothing came of it. We never let it go any further because..." he stopped and glanced over at the door.

Natalie had heard enough, and she took her shopping bags to her bedroom.

"Does Kohl know?"

"I don't know. That happened before Renee knew any of you, including Kohl. She didn't even know his name. It was something that just happened. OK."

Reighanna just sat there, unsure what think. She didn't expect him to have taken her question so seriously. Yet, somewhere in the back of her mind, she knew otherwise.

"We had a conversation one night. I told her about your mom, and she told me a few things about her past. Later that night, things happened."

"So..." Reighanna stopped for a second and decided not to say anything else.

"Reighanna, you're almost eighteen, an adult, and this is a good time to show it. I'm trusting that you will keep this to yourself."

Several seconds had passed before either one of them spoke.

"We may be performing at the new Performing Arts Theater on opening night. We are using a few songs that we left out on previous albums. I'm going to ask Kohl to play piano on a few of them."

She kissed her dad on the cheek. "Kohl will add that certain something that was missing in your music," she said jokingly. "I love you, dad." And she went inside the house.

For the rest of the week Reighanna avoided Renee as much as possible, and if she did run into her, she wouldn't speak to her. Eventually, Renee asked Natalie about her attitude, and even said something to Kohl, but he blew it off with a 'teenagers' comment. But not Renee, she knew something was up. And as Dyllon would put it, if there is something Reighanna can cause drama about, she will.

Chapter Twenty-eight

The following weekend, Reighanna was studying for a rigid math test on Monday. It was her senior year, and she wanted to stay on the top honor roll status. She tapped her pencil on the dining room table as the math questions were just a blur. She couldn't get the conversation she had with her dad off her mind, and now she regrets talking to him.

Moments later, she saw her grandma Natalie sitting in the family room.

"Hi," Natalie said, as Reighanna sat down next to her. "Everything ok? You have been to yourself all week, hardly talking to anyone."

Reighanna leaned her head on her shoulder. "Are we alone?"

"I think so. Renee is out running, Kohl is at work, and Dave is taking a nap. I believe your dad is in the studio, and your brother is with Tyler. Something on your mind?"

Reighanna wanted to talk about what her dad had told her,

but she couldn't because she had promised her dad that she wouldn't tell anyone. "No. I need to get back to my homework."

Natalie knew better because she wouldn't have asked her. "Reighanna, I think I know what's got you. I accidentally overheard you talking to your dad the other day."

Reighanna quickly raised her head up, shocked. "You heard the whole conversation."

"Most of it. The door was ajar, and that's how I heard the two of you talking,"

In the meantime, Kohl came in from work and hung his coat up in the hallway. He then went to the fridge for a coke and saw the two of them talking in the family. But no sooner than he went to join them, he made an abrupt stop upon hearing what they were talking about.

"Even the part about he and Renee sleeping together?"

Kohl kept quiet and slipped over to the counter so that they couldn't see him.

"I heard you ask him if he had feelings for Renee and if they had slept together," Natalie said to her. "That's when I left."

Natalie was just as upset, but even more so for Reighanna. Even though she asked Jaylon about his feelings for Renee, he could have said things differently. That was a huge thing to place on a teenager's shoulder, let alone expect her to keep quiet about it.

"I'm sorry, honey," was all that Natalie could think to say to her.

"I need to get back to my studying."

Kohl turned and darted down the hallway, and to the front room only to run into Dave.

"Hi. You're home early."

Kohl didn't reply and went back to the kitchen. At the same time, Jaylon came in from the studio, and Renee came in from running.

"Wow. It's a family affair," Jaylon sang. "What a coincidence. We're here at the same time." Nobody laughed. "Ok. Something is up with you guys."

"Yeah. Like an affair between you and my wife," Kohl spouted.

"What!" Renee spouted back as she set her keys and phone on the counter.

"You both know what I am talking about."

"We never had an affair. Where did all this come from?" Jaylon asked aggravated.

"I came home just in time to hear Reighanna talking to mom about it."

Jaylon and Renee glance at Reighanna.

"This is what your problem has been all week?" Renee asked.

"So, it's true?" Kohl said.

"I'm not talking about this in front of everyone."

"It's out in the open now."

"It wasn't an affair. It was just a night. This happened before I met any of you. I didn't even know your names, and I never saw any pictures of you guys. I never brought this up because I had let it go. We both knew it wasn't to happen again. That's all there was to it."

Right then, Natalie and Dave joined them. Dave knew something was wrong by the stark look on Kohl's face, and how Jaylon leaned back against the counter with his arms crossed and his lips pressed together like they were glued shut.

"And you didn't think this was something I needed to know?" Kohl asked, trying not to raise his voice.

"What's going on?" Dave asked.

"Kohl overheard a conversation between mom and Reighanna," Jaylon said while darting a cold look at Reighanna. "Something that was supposed to have been kept quiet."

Natalie gasped. "Oh my! I'm sorry Kohl. I thought we were alone."

"Kohl, I'm not sure what all you heard, but I'm sure Reighanna didn't repeat it quite right," Jaylon said like it was no big deal.

"Really. Wow," was all Kohl could say.

Dave finally understood just what they were arguing about, and said, "Ohhh."

"I know I should have told you about Jaylon and me, but with the drugs and all, I let it go," Renee said. "And it happened way before I knew anything about you."

She tried to touch his arm, but he moved away from her and then went to their bedroom.

Dave nodded at Renee. "Maybe you should go talk to him."

Renee grabbed one of Kohl's mixed vodka drinks from the fridge and left the room, and Jaylon went back to the studio.

Dave looked at Reighanna, disgusted. "You couldn't think of anything else to use for your drama excitement? Way to go."

Kohl sat slouched over on the edge of the bed with his hands clasped on top of his knees. And as she sat down beside him, he said, "I thought we had always been upfront with each other about everything. I guess I was wrong. You didn't think I should have known about this from the start of our relationship?"

"I didn't know who you were then. So, how could I?"

"Then? What about when you found out I was his brother?"

"Kohl so much had happened before I met you. That night was left in the dust, and it was never brought up again until much later. And then, when I tried to talk to him about it, he blew it off. I'm sorry. But honestly, as I said, I never gave it any thought. When I met you, I fell head over heels for you, and nothing else mattered. Including my past."

"You're past. You hid that from me for quite a while."

"I didn't hide it from you. You know that," she said through clenched teeth.

"I need some time to let all this set in and not make any rash decisions."

"Rash decisions? Kohl, I love you, and I have loved you since the first time I saw you."

"Just leave me alone," he said sternly.

It was no use saying anymore. He was done talking.

As she started to walk out the door, he asked, "Do you have feelings for him?"

"No."

She shut the door behind her, walked to the front room to avoid Dave, Natalie, and Reighanna who were sitting in the kitchen, and then went out the front door.

Reighanna's phone vibrated. She looked at it and then rushed to the studio.

Natalie looked at Dave, upset. "I thought we were alone."

"Natalie, you have done nothing wrong. All of this will work out."

Dave knew in his own wisdom that none of this was anything like it was portrayed, and he said a silent prayer that Kohl would realize this, as well.

Jaylon paced the floor recollecting that afternoon. He then remembered the door being ajar and knew that is how his mom found out.

Reighanna walked into the studio, and tears welled up in her eyes. "Dad, I'm so sorry. I didn't tell anyone. I swear I didn't. I wanted to talk to grandma about it, but I changed my mind because I had promised you I wouldn't."

"It's ok. I know you didn't," he said while hugging her. "That afternoon, when you refilled my coffee mug and brought it back, the door didn't shut completely, and she overheard us talking. If anyone is at fault, it's mine and Renee's for not being upfront with Kohl in the first place. Let's just say our prayers this mess will work out, somehow." And he sighed, frustrated.

"Yeah, but—"

"Reighanna. I had deep feelings for Renee. After that night I felt I had betrayed your mom, and I couldn't deal with it. I wasn't ready for any kind of relationship. Your mom is the only one I ever truly loved and right now, just like then, I don't think I could ever love like that again. I miss her so much."

"Me, too, dad. Me, too."

As she went back into the house, Jaylon noticed Renee standing outside. He wanted to talk to her and try to fix all of this, but he figured he was the last person she would want to talk to right now.

"Kohl is devastated," Renee muttered as she paced the driveway. "I was so stupid for not mentioning all this to him. Stupid!"

She took the last swig of the vodka drink and then shook the bottle, thinking there might be one more sip left. But another sip wasn't going to numb this mess. She tossed the bottle in the front lawn and took off running towards downtown.

She stopped on a street corner and noticed a bank across the street. She felt the back pocket of her running pants and pulled out her debit card, which she carried with her on long runs in case she needed to buy a bottle of water. She withdrew two-hundred dollars from the ATM and then bought a cheap cell phone at a convenience store that was a block south from the bank.

Her fingers were so numb from the cold that she couldn't feel the buttons on the phone. And then the phone slid out of her hand and right into the snow.

"Just Great!" she spat, shaking the snow off it. "I'll be lucky if this thing works now." She tried making a call. "Come on, work!"

After way too many rings, Ricky answered with a hateful, "Make it quick!" His tone of voice threw her off, so she didn't say anything to him.

He breathed heavy into the phone and muttered a few course words. But before he hung up, he looked at the caller I.D., but he didn't recognize the number. He thought for a second, and a snide grin came across his face, and he laughed under his breath. "Well, if it isn't my little girl," he said as he blew smoke into the phone. "My sweet Renee. I knew you would be calling again. I suppose you want your usual."

"Where can I meet you?"

"At an empty warehouse along the waterway, not too far from your favorite pub. You will know it by the tin roof."

Her teeth chattered hard, and she said, "I'll be there in thirty minutes, if not sooner." She hung up, erased the number off the phone, and threw it into a nearby trash can.

As she walked to the warehouse, she looked up into the sky as the stars were making their debut, but not one star stood out as a sign of hope to nudge her way back home. But then, this recovering addict's legs were hanging off the wagon and with both feet dragging the ground. So, a star of hope, or crying out to God for help, was pointless to her.

In the meantime, Kohl had settled down enough for Renee's words to sink in. And as he paced back and forth, he remembered the second time they met. Renee didn't have a clue who he was, so how could she have known he was Jaylon's brother? It wasn't until the day they moved into the house, when they ran into each other, that everything came into play.

"I have overreacted, to some extent," he said, reasoning with himself. "Yes, Renee should have told me, but she fell in love with me way after the fact. What have I done? I shouldn't have said what I did. I've got to talk to her."

Dave was in the family room watching the evening news when he heard Kohl ask, "Where's Renee?"

"She is outside. I would have thought she'd come back in by now," Dave said concerned. "Too cold to be outside with no coat on. I know she has her running clothes on, but still."

Kohl looked out the front window, and then he looked out the kitchen window, with no luck of seeing her. He then ran to her room upstairs, but she wasn't there, either.

He hurried downstairs and barged into the studio. "Where's Renee?" he demanded.

"I don't know. I saw her outside a while ago," Jaylon said.

Kohl went back into the kitchen and saw her cell phone and keys lying on the counter, and he grabbed them. When he turned to leave, he came face to face with Jaylon.

Jaylon saw the anger in Kohl's eyes. He started to speak, but he kept quiet, not wanting to fuel the flame.

"Why didn't you tell me about this while Renee and I were dating?" Kohl said, trying to stay calm.

"If you can recall, I didn't know who she was seeing until the day we moved here. Several times I tried to get her to tell me who you were. She was very private in that sense, and I respected that, just like she respected my privacy. By the time I found out it was you, you two were so in love and beyond happy. I wasn't going to ruin that for either of you, especially you."

Just then, Kohl heard the evening news anchor report that the police may have found the leader of a local drug cartel on the far south side. Suddenly, an ill feeling welled up in the pit of his stomach. He got his coat and headed outside, slamming the door behind him.

"You better go with him," Dave said to Jaylon. "He's way too upset to be driving, and just maybe the two of you can resolve this. We have never had strife in the family, and we are not starting now," he said sternly.

When he heard the kitchen door shut, he said a prayer of faith for Renee's protection, and that she would come home safely because he knew she was going after drugs. He then said another prayer for Jaylon and Kohl.

Kohl opened his car door, and Jaylon came up behind him and put his on hand on it to keep Kohl from shutting it. "Where are you going?" And then it hit him. "You're going to the south side." Kohl's straight-ahead glare was his answer. "Come on. I'm driving."

Kohl gripped the steering wheel for dear life and unable to look at Jaylon. "Do you have feelings for my wife?" he asked, demanding an answer.

"It's too cold to be talking outside. I'm going to the Escalade."

One by one, Kohl's fingers lost their grip, and he followed Jaylon.

"Answer me," Kohl asked as he got inside Jaylon's vehicle, "are you in love with my wife?"

Jaylon sighed hard and looked him in the eyes. "At one

time I had strong feelings for her."

Kohl glared at him as he slammed the door shut.

"Ok. Yes, I loved her, but after that night, I knew I wasn't over Leighanna. I felt like I had betrayed her. Look, I have not told anyone about this, but the next day I felt God's conviction. I'm serious, too. I heard that small still voice saying make me first. That was the first time since Leighanna's death that I knew God was talking to me, and that what happened between Renee and me was wrong."

Kohl kept quiet and looked out the window.

"I have never seen you as happy as you were the day you bought your wedding rings. That is when I thought of having the surprise wedding for you guys. I would never, ever, do anything to separate you two, and that is why I kept quiet. And as far as Renee not telling you, she had a lot to deal with before you even came into existence."

Kohl thought hard about what Jaylon had told him. He put his hand firmly on Jaylon's shoulder, and said, "We better get going. She's not wearing a coat, nor does she have her cell phone. She still has her running clothes on, but even so, she has to be cold."

Jaylon smiled and said, "Again, I'm sorry about all of this."

Chapter Twenty-nine

Renee picked up her stride and crossed her arms against her trying to stay warm, but the clear sky indicated colder temps were coming. Even so, she kept walking until she reached the farthest end of West Bay Avenue where she happened upon a small shopping strip.

A retro clothing store displayed a black scarf and long black cape in the display window. "I'm feeling warm already," she muttered, and she went inside.

The clerk talked on the phone as she rang up Renee's items. She then put them in a bag and said thanks, all without giving Renee a single glance.

As Renee approached the door to leave, she put the cape on, and wrapped the scarf around her neck, and embraced the warmth hugging her body.

She left the store and walked a half block south when she noticed several police cars parked a few blocks down the street, but she gave no thought to them.

Detective Leary had been investigating the drug cartel within the city when Ricky recently became his number one suspect. An unidentified source informed Leary that Ricky was going to be hanging out on the far south side, but they wouldn't say where his exact location would be.

Detective Leary yawned, thinking this night was a waste of time. He then noticed someone crossing the street, and he adjusted the strength of his binoculars to get a closer look.

Sargent Maly radioed Detective Leary. "You see that?"

Renee glanced their way, again.

"Renee MacKie," Detective Leary radioed back.

"Did you say Renee MacKie?" Maly replied.

Leary searched through his phone contacts and found Renee's number. He had heard about her having to go to rehab for drug abuse, so he figured she just might know Ricky, and just maybe she was going to meet him. But at the same time, he hoped that she didn't know him. "If that's the case, then why is out walking in this part of the city and at this hour?" he muttered.

In the meantime, Jaylon and Kohl scanned the streets as they drove. Jaylon turned down West Bay Avenue when Renee's phone rang inside Kohl's coat pocket.

"Detective Leary?" Kohl said, looking at the caller I.D.

Jaylon frowned. "Why is a detective calling her?"

"We are about to find out," Kohl said, and he answered her phone. "Hello."

"I'm sorry." Detective Leary said, not knowing Kohl's voice. "I have the wrong number."

"Maybe not. This is Kohl, Renee's husband."

"I was hoping she would have answered."

"She left for the evening, and she forgot to take her phone with her. Why are you calling her?" And then he remembered meeting him at the diner. "Wait, you are investigating something that concerns her family."

164

He had a hunch that Kohl was leaving something out, so he went with, "Yes. I have some new information. Please tell her to call me ASAP."

"Sure thing," Kohl said and hung up. "Something is going on. We have to find her," he said to Jaylon.

"We will find her," Jaylon assured him. "Even if it means driving along the waterway."

"Just great," Kohl said, getting even more upset. "God, please watch over her."

Detective Leary laid his phone down on the car seat when another call came through. It was from his unidentified source letting him know that Ricky was at a warehouse along the waterway.

Renee wove around the baron streets and dilapidated buildings. She then crossed another street, walked a few blocks north, and right in plain view was the same white car she had seen many times before, and in front of it was a red sports car.

"Ricky? Maly?" she muttered. What does Maly have to do with him? Or maybe it wasn't Maly in the car, she thought. But, she let the thought go because her main focus was on scoring some dope.

Detective Leary radioed the other police. "Follow my lead with caution, and no lights or sirens," he ordered.

As he and Sargent Maly approached the warehouse, they saw Renee going inside.

In the meantime, Jaylon turned south at the last light by the park. "Why would she have anything to do with a leader of a drug cartel?" Jaylon asked Kohl.

"Could be who she got her dope from."

Jaylon then remembered that afternoon when he and Renee were watching the noon news report about a drug cartel, and how intent she was listening to it. He couldn't help thinking that all the signs were there, telling him she had a drug problem, and yet he ignored them.

Dead grass crunched beneath Renee's shoes as she approached a light coming from a doorway. No sooner than she entered the room, a blood-curdling shrill came from a girl standing in the center of the room. Renee's heart jumped, and she took a few steps back while staring at the emaciated girl. She then turned her attention to a guy that stood several feet in front of the girl, and he was holding a gun to his side.

"Well. Well. Well," Ricky sneered. "If it isn't my little girl. Bout time you came back to me." He darted his eyes toward Phil, who stood within arms reach of Renee. "Give her what she came for," he demanded.

The girl then slurred a few words of distaste at Ricky, and pleaded, "I'll pay you. I promise."

Ricky aimed the gun at her. "I'm tired of hearing you!" And he pulled the trigger. The sound of the gun ricocheted against the tin roof as the bullet pierced the center of her forehead.

Detective Leary, Sargent Maly, and the other police were standing outside their cars ready to enter the building. When they heard the gunfire, Detective Leary motioned for them to go inside.

Renee stood frozen with fear as she watched blood pool from the back of the girl's head, saturating her blond hair. She then felt an arm tighten around her chest and a hot metal object pressing against her neck.

"If this gets out, ever, you're next," Ricky spat into Renee's ear. "Only instead of taking your whole family at once, like the first time, I'll start with grandma, and then Dave and Natalie. Next will be Dyllon, and Reighanna, and then the rock star himself Jaylon MacKie, your boss, and the brother of your husband. Kohl's a lucky man to have you every night. He will be next. You're last in line, my sweet Renee."

And just as he started to push her away, Detective Leary and the other cops burst into the room. When he saw Ricky had taken Renee hostage, he ordered the other police to stand down. He hoped they could resolve this without using their weapons.

"Let her go, Ricky," Detective Leary demanded. "Just put the gun down, and we can talk about this."

"Let her go," Phil shouted, taking a step toward Ricky.

"Stay back, or I'll shoot you, too," Ricky shouted.

"I don't care if you shoot me, but just let her go," Phil pleaded.

"No!"

Ricky had such a tight hold on Renee's chest that her ribs begun to hurt. She tried to free herself with her hand, but Ricky jerked her tighter against him, and he lost his stance and fell back against a weak wall causing it to give away. They landed on the ground, and he lost his grip on her. She tried to run from him, but he grabbed her arm, and drug her into a wooded area next to the building.

Detective Leary and the police ran after Ricky. Phil followed them, and Maly was the last one out of the building.

"What's wrong with you? Let me go!" Renee shouted.

"First time is on me," Ricky said.

"Why are you doing this? How do you know my family?" she asked, struggling to get away. And then she realized what Ricky had said her. "You're the other person that killed my family."

He pushed her onto the ground, and kneeled, straddling her. "I can't believe you didn't figure that out sooner. Your husband leaked out information about the mission which made you a liability. Carl Serelley and I watched you and your family for several weeks." He leaned forward so that he was right in her face. She turned her head to keep from tasting the alcohol on his breath. "I got every move you made down, even what time you went to bed. I told Carl to leave you alone because I wanted you for myself."

He touched her face with the back of his hand. She started to speak, but he covered her mouth with his hand. "Shh, don't say a word, my sweet. This is going to be good," he said, and then he tried to kiss her, but she spit in his face. He wiped the spit off and smacked the side of her head with the gun.

She let out a painful scream that turned into rage. She pushed him off her and tried to get away, but he grabbed her legs, and shove her back down on to the ground.

"Get off of me!"

He didn't move.

"Let her go, Ricky," Phil yelled.

Ricky turned his attention to Phil, which allowed her to get free from him.

"Stop right there," Ricky warned, aiming his gun at her as she fled toward Detective Leary.

"No!" Phil shouted, racing toward Renee.

"Stay back, Phil" Detective Leary demanded, but he didn't listen.

Ricky pulled the trigger, and in the same split second of time, Phil pushed Renee down taking the bullet that was meant for her, and Detective Leary returned fire, shooting Ricky in the head. Phil staggered and then fell to the ground, landing beside Renee.

"Hang on, Phil," Detective Leary said, as he radioed for an ambulance.

Renee kneeled beside Phil. "Why did you do that? He could have killed you."

"I wasn't about to let him harm you. If I had known you were going to be here, I would have found a way to tell you not to come. I'm so sorry." He coughed several times as blood filled his lungs. "I'm glad you are ok," he said choking, and he lost consciousness.

In the meantime, Jaylon and Kohl drove along the waterway and saw several police cars parked in front of a warehouse. Jaylon parked a block up from the warehouse which had not been blocked off.

Kohl panicked when he saw Renee sitting beside Phil and Ricky's dead body lying several feet away from her. Without giving any thought that he was running into a crime scene, he made a mad dash toward Renee, and Jaylon went after him to try to get him to stay back.

Detective Leary saw Kohl and Jaylon approaching Renee when one of the police officers aimed his weapon at them, and yelled, "Stop right there!" Detective Leary immediately ordered him to stand down.

"Renee!" Kohl screamed.

She looked up and ran to him, and he pulled her into his arms. Jaylon finally caught up and embraced them.

An ambulance drove onto the grassy area where Phil lay. A lady EMT got out and begun checking his vital signs. "Pulse is weak, and his lungs are filled with blood," she said to the other EMT. She knew Phil was not going to make it, and said, "Take over. I'm going to check on the girl." She walked over to Renee, and said, "That's pretty good-looking gash on the side of your head."

"Is Phil going to be ok?"

"I'm not sure," she said as she cleaned and bandaged the cut. "I think the cut will heal on its own. Just keep it clean. If it gets worse go to the ER or go to your doctor."

"I knew there was something about Ricky the first time I saw him at the dinner," Jaylon said. "I'm so sorry, Renee. I saw all the signs, but I refused to believe that you could be in trouble."

"It's not your fault. If it's anybody's fault, it's Paul's, my late husband. He started all of this."

"It's done and over with," Kohl said, relieved. "Ricky can't hurt you ever again."

"Detective Leary overhead Kohl. He wanted to chew him and Jaylon out for entering a crime scene, let alone that they about got shot, but instead, he said, "He's right. I'm just glad you're alive. Phil was your saving grace."

"He may have saved my life, but my savior Jesus Christ protected all of us tonight."

"Amen," Jaylon said.

"Why don't the three of you go on home. If I need more information, I'll call you."

"Thank you," she said.

"You're welcome."

"Let's go home," Kohl said.

When they turned to leave, Renee took a quick glance at Sargent Maly. He returned a glance and nodded, but he kept his eye on her as they left.

When they arrive home, Kohl grabbed her before she could take another step toward the house and held onto her for dear life. "Thank you, Jesus, for protecting her," he whispered into her ear.

Chapter Thirty
The Following Sunday

Pastor Benny stood behind the podium and said, "God can take all your failures and make them right. He can turn your regrets and your hurts around and help you to move on toward a better future. But all of this takes forgiveness, not only of others but of yourself. See, God forgives and forgets, but we tend to hang on to our mistakes which gets in the way of moving forward. This is where you need to let God take control and let the healing begin. He will guide you through the process while moving you on to a blessed life through him."

"I'm going outside for a few minutes," Renee whispered to Kohl.

Seconds later, he followed her out of the church.

In the meantime, a man sat in a white car parked between two other vehicles just down the road from the church. He cleared his throat and focused his binoculars. "Well, looky there. My sweet Renee and her husband. You look happy and well," he said with distaste.

"Wait up," Kohl said as Renee walked to their car.

"Kohl, I'm sorry. I'm sorry about everything that happened. I know I should have told you about Jaylon and me, but it was nothing like Reighanna portrayed it. At first, I thought I did love him, but after that night, I felt so wrong about it. That's when I knew God was telling me it wasn't right."

Kohl smiled but kept quiet knowing she had more to say.

"When Jaylon mentioned it later, he said he felt wrong about it, as well. We never talked about it again. Ever. And honestly, finding out about my family, the drugs, and then rehab, I never gave it a thought. I'm sorry."

Kohl embraced her tight. "I'm glad you told me, and I want you to know that I never stopped loving you. But it was a huge shock, especially how I heard it. And with Jaylon trying to ease things with his none of this matter anymore attitude didn't help, either. I know that was his way of dealing with it. Even so, it was wrong how it was handled. But it's all out in the open, and you're still here with me. That's what matters."

She smiled, and said, "I'm glad it's all clear now."

As they walked back inside the church, he said, "No wonder you looked at me like you did in the ER."

She knew what he was talking about. "Yep. You and Jaylon have the same eye shape, just different colors, but you two really don't look that much like."

When the service ended, Benny went over to talk to them.

In the meantime, Jaylon was sitting near the back with his kids. He was talking with other church members when he caught a glimpse of the lady EMT that was at the crime scene. He excused himself and went over to her.

She smiled as he walked up to her. "How are you doing?"

Her sweet smile sent a nervous chill through him. He swallowed hard and said, "I'm doing well. We all are."

"By the way, I'm Noel."

"I'm Jaylon. Would you like to go get something to eat with me?" he asked, and then he blushed. "I mean if you are not with someone."

"I'd love to."

Jaylon told his kids to ride back with their grandma and grandpa, and he would be home later. And as he put his hand on the small of her back to lead her out of the church, a little girl walked up to them. Noel said a few things to her, and then she hugged her and kissed her on the cheek. The little girl went back to her parents, and Jaylon led Noel out of the church.

"You think there is something to that?" Kohl asked.

Renee smiled and said, "Just might be. You never know what the future holds. Let's hope its drama free. Reighanna drama free."

"That was a cute little girl. Golden curls and sweet smile," Kohl said as they walked to their car. He then grinned in a hinting way, and she returned a quick smile.

In the meantime, the man in the white car peered through his binoculars watching them drive out of the church parking lot. He followed them from a safe distance and muttered, "I bet you think Ricky was the end to all of the past. I'll get you in due time. By the way, your children miss you."

Kohl came to a stop at the light, and he leaned over and kissed her. "I'm hungry. Let's go find some where to eat."

She chuckled. "You're always hungry."

"Cupcake for dessert?"

Other books by T. Nelson

Book Two
DEAD AS RAIN
A West Bay Novel

Made in the
USA
Lexington, KY